Blessings
at Our Sav̄

[signature]

WORMWOOD AND GALL

The Destruction of Jerusalem and the First Gospel

A novel by RW Holmen

ISBN: 9780463217948

Other Books by RW Holmen

A Wretched Man: A novel of Paul the Apostle

Gonna Stick My Sword in the Golden Sand

Queer Clergy: A History of Gay and Lesbian Ministry in American Protestantism

Visit the author's website at www.rwholmen.com

Cover design by Lance Buckley

Contents

Foreword

On a late summer's day during the reign of Emperor Vespasian, the world seemingly ended for the Hebrew people of Palestine; tens of thousands died as Roman legions torched Jerusalem and demolished the Holy Temple, the very dwelling place of the Lord God Almighty of Israel. As blood-swollen gutters ran red and the smoke of hellfire blackened the sky, where was God? Was there meaning to life? To death?

The cataclysmic destruction of Jerusalem in 70 CE followed nearly a century of restless churning as the long-suffering Hebrews of Judea and Galilee agitated against Roman Imperial oppression. A Galilean, Jesus of Nazareth, was one of many executed as a perceived threat to Roman authority and the Romanizing sympathizers within Jewish society, including aristocratic priests appointed by authority of the Romans.

As the family and friends of Jesus struggled to keep his movement alive after his crucifixion around 30 CE, a Greek-speaking outsider appeared and dared to promote Jesus as a Hebrew messiah to a Gentile (non-Jewish) world. Paul the apostle spread Jesus' good news across the provinces of the Roman Empire but not without encountering imperial hostility while simultaneously offending the sensibilities and traditions of the elders back in Jerusalem. Along with establishing a network of Gentile churches, Paul also wrote letters that became the first documents of Christendom, dating to the period 50-58 CE, and recognized as authoritative for the church by the mid-second century.

Three decades after the crucifixion of Jesus, Paul was executed in Rome by order of Emperor Nero, and so was Peter, foremost among the disciples of Jesus. Meanwhile, back in Jerusalem, Jesus' own brother James (Ya'akov in Hebrew/Aramaic), who led the Jerusalem remnant of

1

Jesus' followers, was executed by order of the High Priest. Their violent deaths marked the passing of the first generation of the church.

This early church history provided the setting for the author's earlier work entitled, *A Wretched Man, a novel of Paul the apostle*. The present work, *Wormwood and Gall*, is the sequel. *A Wretched Man* concluded in the early 60s CE, and *Wormwood and Gall* begins in 66 CE.

By then, the bubbling cauldron of sectarian strife and anti-Roman sentiment was ready to boil over. Zealot revolutionaries took up arms against the vaunted Roman legions; initial successes chased the Romans from Palestine but unleashed internal power struggles and bloodletting of the priestly aristocracy that was believed to be sympathetic to Rome. When the vengeful Roman legions returned, they swept through the Galilee, leaving cities and villages ablaze and the countryside littered with rotting corpses on crosses. Refugees swelled Jerusalem like goats herded to the slaughter pens.

In the spring of 70 CE, the legions set upon Jerusalem and raised their siege engines and ramparts and launched their catapults. As the summer sun spiked hot, the city's defenses weakened, and before autumn arrived, the temple fell on the 9th day of the Hebrew month of Av. Months after the killing and dying finally ceased, winter rains doused the smoldering ruins and washed the blood and ash from the single wall remaining from God's magnificent marble temple.

The Great Roman-Jewish War was a watershed moment--no, more than that, an apocalypse in which the end of the world seemed near--not only for the Hebrew people, but also for emerging Christianity, and *Wormwood and Gall* remembers this oft-forgotten setting for an early, important chapter in the history of the church. Amid death and destruction,

2

the dispirited remnant of the followers of Jesus, who had been awaiting the return of their crucified messiah for four decades, needed encouragement and words of hope. In response, an unknown person compiled the good news narrative that has come to be known as "the Gospel according to Mark," the next document of Christendom following Paul's letters. What is more, this first gospel served as template and principal source document used by the later compilers of the gospels of Matthew and Luke. John, the fourth canonical gospel, came later still from a different stream of tradition. Although a scholarly consensus agrees with this context and chronology for the development of the gospel tradition, not much more is known about the individuals behind the gospels.

Wormwood and Gall is a fictionalized account of the birth pangs of the early church against the background of revolution, civil war, and apocalyptic devastation. This novel's characterization of the gospel's compiler is entirely fictional as history remembers virtually nothing about the actual person behind the gospel compilation--not even his real name. The gospel document does not identify its author. The terminology "the Gospel according to Mark" dates to a 2nd century identification of an associate of Peter, but current scholarship doubts that association. However, for the sake of consistency and familiarity, the novel's principal character shall be named Markos, the Greek form of "Mark".

Scholars have long looked to the "setting in life" as the starting point in analyzing ancient Biblical manuscripts. Although *Wormwood and Gall* fictionalizes the characters behind the compilation of this gospel, the novel attempts to accurately recreate the events, chronology, and apocalyptic milieu of the Great Roman-Jewish War as the setting that influenced the formation of the first canonical gospel, which in turn influenced the later gospels.

Aramaic is a family of language or dialects, closely related to Hebrew, belonging to various Semitic peoples of the eastern Mediterranean and would likely have been the principal spoken language of Jesus and his Galilean followers. However, since the time of Alexander the Great nearly four centuries earlier, Greek had been the written language of the Mediterranean world. The Gospel according to Mark and the entire New Testament were originally scribed in Greek. The name "Jesus" is the English version of "Yeshua" in Hebrew/Aramaic or "Iesou" in Greek. The novel will use "Yeshua" and "Iesou" interchangeably according to the Hebrew/Aramaic or Greek context. The same is true of the key word translated in English as "messiah" (which means "anointed" or "the anointed one"). In Hebrew/Aramaic, the word is "mashiah," and in Greek, it is "christos."

We begin with a lament for Jerusalem that inspires our title:

How lonely sits the city that once was full of people! How like a widow she has become, she that was great among the nations! She that was a princess among the provinces has become a vassal.

*The thought of my affliction and my homelessness is **wormwood and gall**! My soul continually thinks of it and is bowed down within me. But this I call to mind, and therefore I have hope: The steadfast love of the Lord never ceases, and his mercies never come to an end; they are new every morning; great is your faithfulness.*

Lamentations 1:1 & 3:19-22

Beth Horon 66 CE

I have set the crown on one who is mighty, I have exalted one chosen from the people. I have found my servant David; with my holy oil I have anointed him; my hand shall always remain with him; my arm also shall strengthen him. The enemy shall not outwit him, the wicked shall not humble him. I will crush his foes before him and strike down those who hate him. My faithfulness and steadfast love shall be with him; and in my name his horn shall be exalted.

Psalm 89:19b-24

Chapter One

Cold stone walls of a bone box pressed in upon a jumble of thigh bones, ribs, skulls, and tiny ivory bits from fingers and toes. Some were cracked, broken, or chipped--others worn smooth where joints had rubbed together. Here were bones of martyrs: warriors, yes, but also murdered mothers and grandmothers, slaughtered children and grandchildren. Worms had slowly devoured their decaying flesh before these remains had been packed into this bone box, their immediate resting place on the road to eternity. Dozens of the dead, perhaps more, had been squeezed into this one ossuary, and hollow eye sockets of countless skulls stared blankly into nothingness.

Why am I here with them? Am I not flesh and blood? Is death's rot oozing over my own skin? How long before my own bones turn brittle and then into tiny specks of dust? And what comes after that?

A mortal, born of woman, few of days and full of trouble, comes up like a flower and withers, flees like a shadow and does not last.

And what of the blood moon that pours out upon Jerusalem through the night and the smoke that blackens the sun by day? Dust and ash and suffocating fear choke the stale air inside death's chamber, and I labor to breathe. I lick my chalky lips with a thick tongue. Are these the end of days?

I hear a rattle of bone against bone. Do the bones shift? Do restless spirits stir within?

I want to cry out with them, for them ... and, for myself. "No, this cannot be! This must not be!" Certainly, our maker intended more than misery, more than injustice, indeed ... more than death.

Against all reason, I dare to hope, and that is why I have been sent here: to bolster the courage of these forlorn souls, to uplift and inspire, to instill trust and restore meaning even amid death and dying.

I unroll a papyrus scroll of my own making with ink strokes still damp, and I begin to read aloud the words I had writ for this very moment:

The beginning of the good news of Iesou Christos ...

****

I wondered about the one. The one who would be the death of me or I of him. Does God decree who shall live and who shall die? Does God care? Do I care?

I worried that I would not be steady and decisive if it is my fate to do the killing, but it probably won't come to that. I expected to face a battle-scarred veteran, tall and strong and boasting superior Roman weaponry. I unsheathed my hunting knife, my only weapon, and tested its sharpness with my thumb. It was merely a flint tool used to skin animals, and the edge seemed dull to the touch. How could flint stand up to the steel of the Roman *gladius*, the legionnaire's double-edged short sword? My feeble hunting knife was not even a match for the Roman *pugio*, the dagger that hung on the legionnaires' left hip. How could my lamb's wool tunic compare with their mail or scale breastplates or my skull cap with the Roman *galeas*?

Will the one who kills me do so out of loyalty to the emperor or merely because that's what soldiers do? Perhaps he will be cruel with hatred like the zealots I marched with, and he will not dispatch me quickly but draw out my agony. Perhaps the prayer on my lips should be for a painless death.

I slept a fitful sleep. Clouds darkened the sky, and only the trill of the lark said morning was near. Early-winter mist soaked the haunting despondency that followed me to this valley.

"Eat hearty."

The old Galilean's words followed the men in rumpled tunics ambling on stiff legs to this tree or that for their morning piss.

"Twill be hours before you eat again."

Or ever, I thought, as I chewed on a dried-out hunk of flatbread and emptied my sack of rancid dates, but I hungered for my first taste of battle.

By the time gray dawn seeped over the eastern hills, restless energy kept me pacing. I remembered my departed father and the time he allowed me to tag along on a hunt into the mountains. I sensed the same eagerness and anticipation this morning. It was naive, I suppose, but I couldn't deny feeling the sweet boyhood thrill of stalking a deer as we prepared our ambush of the Roman legion.

I was placed with others high atop a hill in the rearmost line. Far to the west, I saw a blue line on the horizon, a glimmer of the Great Sea. Beneath the ridge, the hillside fell away sharply to a winding pathway. In some places, the expected route of the Romans was merely a narrow ledge with a rock face above and a precipice below. Archers huddled behind boulders and clumped in the trees, nervously fingering their bowstrings as they waited to launch their arrows onto the unsuspecting Roman column as it snaked its way along the trail. Our infantry, equipped with darts, spears, and swords, lay in wait in the thick brush around the trail, ready to fling their darts and then charge into the Romans soon after the archers' arrows signaled that battle had begun. Across the rugged gully, vast numbers of

8

additional Galilean zealots mirrored the lines on this side of the ravine, waiting to ambush the Romans in a crossfire.

Thousands of boisterous men--who normally laughed at their own stories, who boasted of their sexual adventures, who teased and taunted each other mercilessly--now paused in suffocating silence. A wren filled the void and proudly repeated her full-throated verse, but several thousand pricked ears failed to hear the birdsong, nor did vigilant eyes heed the darting swallows that dined on the bugs that hovered over the valley. On this day, we only had eyes and ears for the Romans.

"Menachem."

At first, I didn't recognize the false name I had assumed, and I didn't respond.

"Menachem! Are you deaf?"

I jerked my head toward the squad leader.

"Yes, yes, I am here," I sprang to my feet.

The eyes of the grizzled Galilean squinted as he took my measure.

"Lean against this tree and fix your eyes on me. Stay silent and still until you hear my command; then we shall rush down the slopes and into glory."

I was one of the reserves who would be the last to enter the fray. We would either mop up or become the final sacrifice, depending upon how the battle unfolded. Self-doubt swept over me. Would I bravely accept my fate to kill or be killed, or would I slink away and cower my way home to Damascus? I looked for encouragement in the faces of those around me, but it was only fear I saw, and I assumed the skin on my own face was drawn tight against my high cheekbones like the faces that mirrored my own. I had been one of these would-be warriors long enough that I'm sure

I smelled as bad as the worst of them. From the appearance of the others, I suspected my oily black hair lay matted and snarled upon my high forehead, and dust and grime, and maybe a few bread crumbs, flecked my meager, scraggly beard. I wished that I was as strong as these men who worked with their hands, but I had always been slight of build, lacking strength and the nimbleness of an athlete. My own hands were soft and pale, my fingers long and delicate, unlike the callused and weathered palms of these men with broken thumbs or twisted digits.

Before midday, the dust of the approaching Roman army appeared over the hills to the east, and my eyes caught the glint of the sun on countless souls sheathed in armor as they twisted along the trail like an endless shimmering snake. I shivered with excitement. Surely, God had chosen this time to establish his reign on earth, and I would be his holy warrior on this great and terrible day.

Mounted on a tall stallion, our general, Eleazar ben Simon, moved up and down behind the lines, behind the crest of the ridge, and beyond the sight of the advancing Romans. A thick mat of curly red hair and a beard to match framed a ruddy face wrinkled like a raisin. A pink scar from a recent skirmish ran from brow to nose between wide-set eyes. A tall brown turban wound over the top of his head with a loose end flapping in the breeze. I briefly caught the eye of the messianic warrior: deep, dark, savage, and brutal ... yet calculating and confident. His gaze pierced me deeply, and I felt naked and exposed as if he sensed my uncertainties, as if he raised the same questions I asked of myself: "Who are you and why are you here?" Perhaps he would interrogate me later, but now he moved down the line, surveying the scene and offering encouragement and final instructions.

Tucked behind trees, brush, and boulders, the rebel lines lay hidden along the ridge for a mile or more, thousands of farmers and fishermen awaiting Eleazar's battle cry. Mounted brigands brandished swords and waited impatiently behind the ridge. They would form our cavalry, who would ride into the confused and dispirited Romans in a third wave following the volleys of the archers and the charge of the infantry. At least, that was the plan.

In the valley below, the vanguard of the Romans passed by my vantage, followed by wagon loads of war materials and foodstuffs pulled by oxen. Then came an entourage of mounted cavalry that surrounded the legate on his own magnificent stallion that pranced--something between a walk and a canter. Cestius Gallus was resplendent in shining armor, a plumed helmet, and a red cape that could only be silk. I feared he would hear my heart thumping as he passed by, even from afar. His escort boasted similar attire, but his plume seemed taller, his robe redder, and his stallion nobler. The mounted cavalry included the legate's own chosen bodyguards, his Praetorian cohort. As we expected, the narrowness of the trail forced the Romans to pass by in single file rather than in wide columns, and there were no flanking units. An hour earlier, Roman scouts had moved through the pass, but our forces had not been discovered. They said that a Roman legion consisted of more than five thousand troops, and like mindless ants with antennae bobbing, they streamed past the tips of arrows, darts, spears, and swords, unaware they were marching straight toward Hades.

Though I expected it and waited for it, I was startled when Eleazar ben Simon began the bloodletting with a guttural, inhuman cry. The war whoop swelled as it moved from one commander to the next, rolling through the hills in an instant, followed by the twang of bowstrings and the whoosh of a thousand arrows arced high, then five thousand, then ten. Most missed their mark and many more bounced off the armor of the legionnaires, but enough plunged deeply into human and horse flesh to create an instant panic. Hundreds of Romans fell dead or wounded in the archers' first wave of our attack. When our infantry tossed their darts from close range and twirled their slings loaded with stone bullets, hundreds more fell. We cheered from the hilltop as the Romans stumbled about in full-scale disarray when our infantry charged from nearby bushes killing additional hundreds within minutes. Roman commanders attempted to organize their troops to no avail. Overwhelmed by waves of Hebrew infantry, solo legionnaires fought and died alone, and the famous Roman battle formations never materialized. Their artillery was useless. Ballistae with spear projectiles the length of a man and catapults capable of heaving stones the size of a bull's head were never assembled, never loaded, and never fired. By the time our cavalry raced down the slopes, the battle was nearly won.

Then I saw myself; I was running, running, running, toward the battle and not away from it. Fear had given way to bloodlust, and I ran, and I whooped, and I stabbed at the air with my hunting knife as I ran in for the kill.

Chapter Two

The night before this great battle, I leaned against a rock and gazed at the brilliance of the heavens. Our tradition promised that the descendants of Abraham would be as vast as the stars. Under a moonless and cloudless sky, the aura of countless heavenly bodies melted together and became indistinguishable. A chilly evening breeze carried the scent of fresh rain following a short-lived cloudburst that washed over the dusty hillside hours earlier.

Our squad leader made his rounds and set the night watch; I was too new, too fresh, too untested, and so he allowed me to attempt sleep. We teased him by calling him our *decanus*, the term the Romans used for the leader of a unit of ten foot-soldiers. Our *decanus* was a peasant like the rest of this rag-tag band of revolutionaries--common men who banded together to thieve from the Romans and their lackeys: the tax collectors, priests, and boot-licking aristocrats. The Romans called this sort "brigands," and the Galileans bore the name with pride.

"They stole from us," the farmers and fishermen turned thieves turned rebels often reminded themselves, "and we are just taking our money back."

Our squad leader was older than most of us, his fiftieth summer well behind him, and he wore a skull cap over the peak of his bald head. Tufts of mottled black and gray hair puffed out along the sides. A bent nose presided over a sad face and a short beard. His rumpled, sweat-stained tunic was standard uniform for this militia. He spoke slowly and softly, much like his ambling gait, but when he shared his personal story, his jaw jutted out, and the words vomited from deep in his gut.

"First the tax collector demanded the eggs from our laying hens, but then he came and lopped off the head of our rooster and claimed the bird for his own pot. The bastard departed on blood-splattered legs as the wings of the carcass flapped in protest.

The old man's growl grew louder and quicker.

"Then he took the freshly-shorn lamb's wool, then he stole our goat cheese, and finally he returned to herd the ewes away to his own flock."

"'Do something,' my old wife pleaded, but what could I do?"

His eyes clouded, and a single tear tracked down a wrinkled cheek and disappeared into his scowl.

"The last day he came with half a dozen of his Roman friends, a centurion and his legionnaires. When they killed our milk cow and butchered and roasted it right in front of us, leaving us with the entrails, my eldest son seethed with rage, but I held him back; it would do no good to orphan his children and my grandchildren. That night, we sent the womenfolk and the children to take refuge with my brother-in-law, and my sons and I stole away into the hills to join the brigand leader, Simon's youngest son named Eleazar, but not before flinging a burning stick into the tax collector's granary."

We sat silently for a few moments, and then I detected a slight upward curl at the corners of his lips.

"We watched from a nearby ridge as the flames leapt higher and higher," he said, "and my nose caught the pleasant scent of burning grain."

When the old man ambled away, I puzzled on my own story. Why was I here? I was different. I was not from the Galilee like most of this rabble; I was an educated man from the city of Damascus. Though this ancient oasis city was not far away, less than a fortnight astride a swift

14

horse, it was not a Jewish city, and Gentiles far outnumbered the Jewish populace. My Aramaic dialect differed from the speech of these rough Galileans, and I kept my mouth shut for fear of discovery that I was an outsider and my loyalties questioned. I worried that I might let a Greek word or phrase slip out. You see, I was a scribe, and Greek was the language of the lettered few, the vocabulary of diplomacy and poetry, and the parlance of commerce and industry. I had scribed contracts, inventories, and letters, for which I had been well-paid, but to these zealots from the Galilee, Greek was the tongue of the hated foreigner from across the Great Sea, the oppressor, the occupier, the ones whose blood would purge God's holy land of the infestation of evil.

My own name betrayed me. "Markos" was Greek, not a solid Hebrew name like the ones that identified the Galileans on this hillside. "Marcus" was Roman—worse yet. So, I lied and called myself "Menachem." The men of this rebel army could neither read nor write, but many could trace a single letter with a stick in the sand to signify their name. At least my "M" was honest.

Why was I here? Why had I left the peaceful and well-paid existence of a scribe in my home in Damascus? Why was I prepared to do battle and perhaps die with a smelly band of revolutionaries who have the temerity to take on imperial Rome and the Legion XII, the so-called Thunderbolt Legion that had marched down from Antioch of Syria to teach the rebellious Jews a lesson? True to their reputation, the Legion left stinking Jewish corpses rotting in their path.

The cause of the Galileans was just, that I believed. It was the thirteenth year of the reign of Emperor Nero, and when word reached Damascus that the long-simmering cauldron had finally boiled over, that there had been an uprising in Jerusalem and the Jews had thrown off the yoke of their Roman masters, it seemed that the long-awaited reign of God was near. I wasn't the only son of Abraham to join God's army upon hearing this good news. The God of the Jews was my God, and I hoped in the promises of the prophets of old that God would deliver his people. I was one of the stars scattered across the heavens, and I would follow the leader that rose up, the anointed son of God, the mashiah who would scourge the land of evil and restore God's reign on earth. Someday, the lion would lie down with the lamb as the prophets foretold, but tomorrow would not be such a day. Tomorrow would be for killing and dying.

Was Eleazar ben Simon the man God had anointed? He was our leader, the counterpart to the Roman legate Cestius Gallus who slept nearby on silk pillows in an ornate linen tent at the head of the pass of Beth Horon. Had God chosen a filthy peasant from the Galilee, a ruthless brigand whose thievery swelled into full-fledged rebellion? Who could know?

Why was I here? This political answer, this cause of rebellion against the Romans, was true enough and righteous, and this was my stated explanation, but there were those who doubted. I, myself, was the chief doubter for I suspected there was a deeper purpose that I could not grasp. Let a silly riddle be my answer, at least for now. My reason for being here was that I sought a reason for being here. My purpose was to find a purpose. My motive was to find motivation. I have lost hope, my life seemed meaningless, and I have come to Beth Horon seeking to regain what I have lost, but I also wondered; was I seeking death to stanch my heartache as my mother worried?

16

I rumpled up my goatskin bag and wedged it behind my neck as I sprawled under the vast sky. Even with arms spread wide, I couldn't span the edges of the heavens--north or south, east or west--all corners of the cosmos lay beyond my fingertips. A flaming star arced past and then was gone.

I have always been a star-gazer. Many nights I slept atop the thatched roof of my mother's home in Damascus, bathed in heaven's light until bleating goats announced the arrival of a new day. Mother would be there in the cramped, walled-in courtyard alongside our mud-brick house--did she ever sleep? --milking the dams, stoking the charcoal to bake her flat loaves, or beating the rugs that warmed the dirt floor of the main chamber of our home. I basked in the last flickers of the morning star and arose only when the aroma of fresh-baked bread wafted up to the rooftop.

But that was then, and now I slept in a faraway place. I separated myself from the others and tried to rest in tall grass. When I shut my eyes, I heard my own breathing mingling with the night sounds of unseen creatures in the air, the trees, and the sod. I drew a deep breath and let the night air out slowly. The sounds of solitude comforted me for the moment. I drew another delicious breath, and another, carrying the mixed scents of moldy leaves, horse dung, or a wisp of smoke from the nearby Roman campfires.

The respite wouldn't last. They never did. I drifted off, but then a snatch, a whisper, perhaps a bleating goat from a nearby hillside intruded into my dreams as a shrill baby's cry, and I awoke shivering yet sweating. For a moment, my breaths were short and quick as my consciousness chased the nightmare.

Chapter Three

As war whoops erupted from my breast, and I rushed down the slope into battle, I was a timeless warrior, at one with the soldiers of past and future, those dead and those yet to be born, caught in the eternal fate of humankind to kill or be killed.

Just as I reached the trail, I stumbled and smashed my knee on a jagged rock. I sniffed about on my hands and knees, and when I found my flint knife and stood, I saw a Roman soldier watching me with puzzlement. An arrow protruded the neck of his dead roan mare. The Roman could have killed me as I muddled about like a dog, but he merely sat on the ground clutching an object in his hands, holding it close to his breast like a lost child. In the din and confusion of battle, I took a step toward him, and he bent over the object, clutching it tighter, but he gave no hint of self-defense. Why didn't he stand and fight? I saw no wound. His *gladiu*s remained sheathed on his right hip, his *pugio* on his left. When I took another step, he bowed his head to shield the object.

With my knife in my right hand, I grabbed his hair with my left and jerked his head back. Tears tracked down his dusty cheek, and he mumbled in Latin, which I did not understand, and I replied in Greek.

"You are my prisoner." I held my knife aloft in a threatening manner.

"No, no," he replied in Greek. "You must kill me. Please, you must kill me. I am humiliated."

The blood-gorged beast of battle was all around me, and in me, and was me. The man at my mercy was *the* enemy even if he was not *my* enemy, and without thought, or malice, or will, I did what soldiers do. When he threw his head back to expose his neck, I mindlessly raked my knife across his throat, and his blood squirted in my face, onto my tunic, and over my sandals.

I staggered back and stumbled over the dead horse and sat upon the poor beast. For a moment, the Roman stared at me and into me and beyond me. I watched stupefied as dark red blood, almost black, pulsed from his neck, then slowed and stopped. His eyes grew vacant, seeing what I could not. In that moment, I thought of many persons I had known, now dead, and I wondered if he saw them. Did the faraway look in his eyes behold his own wife in Rome, or Macedonia, or any of a thousand places? Did he see his children? Did he see them crying at the news of his noble death in battle, fighting and dying for the glory of Rome? Suddenly, I wanted to talk with the man:

What is your name? Tell me of your family. What are your children's names? What foods do you like? Isn't this a fine day? I'm sorry about your roan mare.

With a slight convulsion, he slumped backwards, and his life was over. Lifeless hands released the object, and it tumbled into a bloody puddle. I vomited all over myself and the dead mare. Though there were thousands around me as the battle raged, I heard nothing and saw nothing except a man dead by my own hand. I had gone from calm, to energetic, to fearful, to exhilarated, to bloodthirsty, and now I sat in the sticky squalor of his blood and my vomit. It was an awful moment and yet profound, absurdly spiritual and evil, holy and unholy, sacred and vile. Did this death hold meaning? I was a soldier, yes, and he was a casualty of war, but I was also a sacrificial priest, and this had been a ritual killing, Was I also a murderer?

Slowly I remembered that I still lived, and I picked up my knife, wiped the blood on the hide of the roan mare and slid the flint blade into its sheath. I reached for the blood-smeared object the Roman had clutched so dearly. It was a statuette, an eagle with wings spread in menacing fashion, and it was solid gold. A jagged, broken stub of wood protruded from the bottom.

At first, I was confused, and then realization hit me like a boulder had dislodged and rolled into my chest. The soldier I killed was the *aquilifer*, the one with the high honor of bearing the *Aquila*--the legion's standard, the very symbol of Roman might—perched high atop a wooden pole. I looked around, but no one had noticed. I was stunned, and I collapsed on the dead horse again as the killing and the dying wound down. I wiped the bloody *Aquila* with my tunic, and stuffed it into my goat-leather bag, which I clutched tight, much like he had done, the Roman *aquilifer* whose life I ended.

The victorious rebel mob jabbed swords and spears into the Roman wounded. There would be no prisoners, except for a few officers who would face their own humiliation. It was a rout, and a Roman legion had been decimated, not merely defeated, but destroyed. It would be a day that history would long remember, the worst defeat inflicted on the Romans since the founding of the Empire. Only a few escaped, apparently including the legate, whose body was not found among the dead. No matter, he would live the remainder of his days in disgrace.

The shouts swelled as the dead Romans were stripped of their weaponry. When the next battle would come, as it surely would, Eleazar's army would be equipped with the finest weapons the world had known: Roman swords, spears, shields, armor, ballistae, catapults, darts, javelins, and composite bows of horn, wood, and sinew, together with long straight arrows with the finest fletching. Disassembled artillery pieces were found in ox carts. More whoops and cheers as sacks full of gold and silver coins were discovered in large oaken chests. Eleazar's rabble had become a formidable army with the means and the materiel to better any foe.

Many a bonfire lit up the sky that night, and more war booty--casks of wine and barley beer--fueled dancing, singing, and boasting. I was still numb, but I felt I must speak to Eleazar, and I limped from one fire to the next seeking our heroic leader. A jagged wound across my right knee, split open and mangled when I tumbled in the rocks, slowed my search. I hobbled along among the revelers until I found our victorious general.

I had heard stories of the rape of a defeated enemy, of forced sexual penetration of a man by a man, and now I witnessed it. A captured officer of the defeated Roman legion knelt on all fours as Eleazar humped him from behind. Whoops of encouragement filled the night sky. The subjugation ritualized the totality of the conquest for the victors and the utter defeat for the vanquished. Here was the sin of Sodom: rape as assertion of power, control, and domination. When Eleazar finished, the humiliated man who was no longer a man crawled into the shadows, taunted by jeers from the Galileans. One of the few survivors of our ambush would live the remainder of his life wishing he had been among the battle dead.

Eleazar snatched up the Roman's *galeas* and placed it askew atop his own head. The helmet's broken plume hung limply down the side.

"More beer!" Eleazar bellowed with arms extended skyward.

His men hooted.

21

Eleazar drained a goblet before he staggered back and sat upon the bed of a Roman ox cart. The beast of burden lay dead and tangled in the leather harness. Toast after toast was raised high in honor of the Galilean general who delivered the victory over the oppressor of God's people. Eleazar ben Simon. The mashiah. The anointed one. The son of God.

I gathered my courage before I dared approach. When I did, bodyguards cut me off, but when I pulled the *Aquila* from my bag, they parted like the Red Sea and bade me forward. I presented the Roman standard to Eleazar who didn't seem to understand, at first. Then his eyes lit up, and his chin dropped. He awkwardly climbed atop the cart and held the *Aquila* high over his head, and the loudest cheers of the night reverberated through the hills. Then, he reached down and pulled me onto the cart, and together we raised the *Aquila* aloft once more.

I'm not much of a beer drinker, but someone handed me a Roman goblet filled to overflowing with froth running down the sides. I barely remember the back slaps and the many goblet refills as I became a hero, the personification of the spectacular victory. My blood-stained tunic added legitimacy, as did the wound on my leg.

I didn't mention the vomit.

In that moment, my name was Menachem, and I forgot who I was.

Chapter Four

Invisible clouds scudded across the night sky, swallowing the starlight in patches of blackness. When I slept, I heard the screams, but when I awoke, silence pressed against my chest, and I labored to breathe. The wailing within my nightmare was always the same: the moaning of dying soldiers would mingle together and become a baby's cry, and when the child's sobbing stopped, I would awaken with a start to crushing quiet.

Morning mist brought the stench of burning flesh and searing pain in my knee. Whether it was the day-after effects of the barley beer or the noxious odor of dead bodies being consumed by a raging fire, I gagged and choked and heaved my insides out. When they doled out stale bread, my stomach twisted again. My heroic status didn't prevent my squad leader from assigning me, along with countless others, the task of gathering up the dead to be burned. There were purely practical reasons for disposing of the bodies, but I couldn't help but think that we now made burnt offerings of the blood sacrifices of the previous day.

Again, I wondered. Why was here, why was I killer and not killed, why was I hailed as hero when I felt myself to be a villain? If I sought death, why was I alive? Why did God torment me?

Back home in Damascus, I took a wife from a leading Damascus family, and I invested her generous dowry on an exterior staircase, replacing the wooden ladder, and I built a two-room addition atop the roof of my mother's home--a bedroom for my mother who would move upstairs and a *tablinum* for me where I would receive my clients and conduct my growing and prosperous trade as a scribe.

Our marriage was arranged, but love bloomed in the spring. My bride was a young thing and delicate like a pale, pink rose, and my heart warmed

23

on the day she whispered that she carried our child. Her cheeks were flush and full, and her wide brown eyes danced as she held my hand to her belly, so I could also feel the life stirring within her. But, it had not gone well for her from the start, and the grim frown on the midwife's face at the start of delivery told me more than I wanted to know.

As the women did what women do in such times, I waited in my *tablinum* upstairs, but I couldn't stay confined, so I climbed atop the rooftop and paced. When the noonday sun turned blood-red, a howling desert wind rushed in from the east, muffling a single, shrill scream from the room below. Grit pricked at my face, and my skull cap disappeared in a swirl of flying sand, but as suddenly as the dust devil arrived, it departed. As I crawled about on all fours searching for the reed pen that was missing from behind my ear, I heard the bawling of a newborn signifying life, and hope, and eternity, but before my face could break into the broad grin of a proud father, I realized I merely heard the bleating of the goats in the courtyard, and I was alone, swallowed up in numbing silence. I choked on the chalky dust that hung in the hot, still, timeless air. My wife, my child, my future, my hopes, my aspirations, and my identity were whisked away by the capricious breeze. I was no longer who I had been. The whirlwind sucked up my life, and I came to dread the dawn and the bawling of the lambs.

At first, I insisted there was no violence in my hands, and my prayer was pure. Yet, my face was red with weeping. Morning and mourning brought no light, and I came to know the terror of deep darkness. The why of it all tormented me, and I became convinced that I must not be blameless. Along with everything else, the whirlwind had stripped away

24

my skin and bone and exposed my shame. How else could my great pain be explained?

And so, I escaped to Beth Horon only to wander in this valley of dead souls. With the stink of burning flesh all around, with blood and vomit caked to my tunic, my agony was not relieved; to the contrary, my despair only increased as my shame was verified and stirred in with my grief in an unholy stew. Grief is sorrow, an emptiness, a deep heartache. The worst thing about grief is that it lingers, and I had not recovered yet; now, the abject and immediate terror of dealing with the dead and remembering my own bloodthirsty role in yesterday's carnage brought me not to the reign of God but to a living death. The contorted face, the vacant eyes, and the spurting blood of the man who died at my hand haunted me, and each lifeless body I carried to the fire stoked the flames of damnation. There was cruel irony in the adulation I received from others for an act that revealed my great shame to myself. There is no judgment that cuts as deep as self-condemnation, and the praise that was heaped upon me only salted the wound.

I soon discovered that my wineskin muted the pangs of self-reproach. As the battle slipped into the past, one sunset at a time, the horror receded into a dull despondency; perhaps the accommodation I reached with my shame and the lie that I became was a sign of the increasing rot within. I was no less guilty, but I felt less guilty, and perhaps that was the greater sin.

Each day we were joined by others who now dared to be part of our movement. With victory, many found the courage to believe, and our ranks swelled as the news soared on the winds throughout Judea and Galilee and beyond. The Romans had been expelled from God's holy land, and God's

25

people were free again. Many others frequented our camp, not to join but to celebrate. Village folk from all around came bearing gifts of cheeses, wine, mutton, and fresh loaves, still warm from the hearth. Painted women came, and for just a few shekels, they disappeared with a soldier for a dalliance in the grass. The festive mood persisted in the days that followed as Eleazar and his commanders began to plan our triumphal march to Jerusalem. Important men came from Jerusalem and whispered with Eleazar and his confidantes. For now, we cared for our wounded and regrouped.

Rumors persisted that King Herod Agrippa II, the great-grandson of Herod the Great, had fled Jerusalem and taken refuge in the Greco-Roman city of Caesarea Philippi located in the far north of the Galilee not far from my own city of Damascus. Hah! Hardly surprising that the king, nurtured with the princes of Rome and appointed to his throne by the emperor, should show his true colors. A day of reckoning lay ahead for his aristocratic friends in Jerusalem!

For now, the tales grew taller, not the least of which was my own.

"How many did you kill to capture the eagle?"

"Only one."

"Hah! I heard it was a dozen of the legate's own Praetorian guards."

"Well, maybe half a dozen," I replied.

"Was it a lance or a sword that gashed your leg?"

"I couldn't say. I was occupied with my own slashing."

It seems a movement requires a mythology, and I was hard-pressed to deny the stories that swirled around me, much less live up to the heightened expectations. One evening, I swallowed more than my fill of fresh wine. Two of my drinking companions briefly left our campfire circle and soon returned with three giggling women dressed in brightly-colored garments.

"This one is for you," said the hulking Galilean. "Or, do you want all three?"

The tallest of the women, with her black hair bunched atop her head and mulberry juice rouge painted on her cheeks, leaned over to pull me to my feet, nearly spilling her breasts. Too easily, I submitted and followed along into the brush, thankful for the darkness when we left the aura of the campfires and oil lamps. Once in the conifer shrubs, my whore lifted her robes, spread her legs, and I entered, assuming, or at least hoping, that she could not feel that my member inside her was not circumcised. After a minute or two of clumsy thrusting and groping, nothing happened, and then I went limp.

"Oh, Sweetie, it happens, just let me rub it."

I bolted back to the camp.

"Menachem, Eleazar summons you." A few days after the battle, the command came from a burly man in an ill-fitting Roman *cuirass* harvested from the dead.

I was numb to the words. I didn't have the energy to wonder or worry, and I mindlessly followed Eleazar's messenger. Guards pulled back the tent flaps, and I stepped into Eleazar's lair. The Galilean general's snake-charming gaze transfixed me as he took my measure. Alarm began to seep into my bones. Perhaps he knew more about me than I had dared to share.

First, there was the matter of my bloodlines. I wasn't about to mention that my grandfather on my mother's side had been an anonymous

27

Roman solder. I never understood why my mother wasn't embarrassed about that nor did she seem to care that her own birth mother had been a whore to the Roman garrison in Damascus. My prostitute grandmother had sold her infant daughter to a loving Jewish woman who named her Charis and raised her as her own child. My mother had been raised as a Jew and married my Jewish father, but I worried that I wasn't pure enough for these Gentile-hating Galileans whose rebellion I had joined.

Nor had I been circumcised on the 8th day like a proper Jewish male child. You see, my parents were Hellenists--Greek-speaking, Diaspora Jews who were lax in their observance of Hebraic law known as Torah; we didn't always eat the right foods, nor did we observe the Sabbath and the festivals with appropriate reverence. "Hellenist" implied "Greek," and when the zealots mouthed the word, they wrinkled their nose and spit it out like they were swearing. My uncut flesh provided the most damning evidence of my Hellenistic shortcomings. If my deficient manhood would be discovered, my fealty to the zealots' cause might be questioned, and I would be in danger. And so, I pissed alone.

But, today would not be the day of my unveiling; instead, Eleazar meant to leverage my hero's status for his own purposes. With a snort, Eleazar turned away and muttered, "Menachem, you shall command ten new recruits. They need a man with cunning and bravery to lead them." I heard his thick sarcasm even if his lieutenants did not.

After I was placed in charge of my own stitched-leather tent (another spoil of war) that slept ten men in shifts, promotions came in swift succession; I was soon in command of five such tents and fifty men, mostly new arrivals who thrilled at the stories and eagerly looked forward to their own taste of blood on the battlefield. Such is the folly of the innocents.

Rehum, one of the new arrivals placed in my charge, was known to me and me to him, and I again feared that my secret would be revealed to Eleazar ben Simon and the others. I saw him before he saw me, and I quickly moved to his side.

With my hand on his shoulder, I whispered, "Call me Menachem. Please call me Menachem."

"Menachem," he said, but his eyes narrowed and darkened. "Menachem," he said again, more softly, almost as a whisper.

Rehum also hailed from Damascus, but he was not of my circle of Hellenistic Jews nor did he frequent the synagogue of my parents that followed the so-called but crucified christos, Iesou of Nazareth. Rehum was from a strict Torah-abiding synagogue that scrupulously followed the Hebraic law, but he didn't question me or my Hellenistic background--not yet, at least. He was about my age, mid-twenties, but he was thicker and fitter than me. His black beard was crisp and manicured, and I envied his confident manner even as I worried about his inscrutability. He didn't say much unless you spoke directly to him, and then he put his answer clearly and with a matter-of-fact certainty.

"What news of Damascus?" I asked.

"Many Jews in Damascus have been killed by Romans in reprisal for the humiliation of Beth Horon," he said without emotion. "Synagogues have been torched."

The sun was low in the western sky, and I had taken no midday meal other than half a wineskin. His words dried up my muddle, and instant

29

alarm for the mother I left behind slammed my thoughts with stone-cold sobriety.

"What, what about …?"

I stammered and could not spit out my fears, but Rehum anticipated my question.

"The synagogue of the Hellenists still stands," he said.

I couldn't discern whether he spoke with disgust or merely dispassion.

"And my mother? She's the synagogue leader, you know."

Rehum leaned over to pick up his kit, signaling that he wished our conversation to end.

"Your mother is well, so far as I know," he said as he turned to leave. "Which is more than I can say for my own brother who suffered the wrath of the Roman vigilantes."

Slowly my breathing returned to normal. Of course, I was glad that Mother was safe, but I also felt guilty. I was joyful that it was others and not my mother who suffered Roman retribution, and for that I was ashamed.

With the news of the reprisals in Damascus, I understood the empire-wide tremors emanating from our earthquake in the pass of Beth Horon. Surely, our rout of the Romans had not been the end but merely the beginning. The Romans would not, could not, accept rebellion in the provinces. Yet, this realization didn't frighten Eleazar, his lieutenants, or the mass of troops under their command; instead, God's army welcomed further confrontation that would lead to total victory.

Eleazar ben Simon's own status also swelled following the battle of Beth Horon. Camp talk labelled him the mashiah, and it was hard to argue differently. Indeed, he had been the warrior who delivered God's people and God's land from the oppressor. He appeared to be precisely what the prophets promised and what generations of Jews had expected. Could anyone doubt that the massive victory at Beth-Horon had not been God ordained? Indeed, this had been God's victory, and Eleazar had been his instrument. Eleazar believed, no less than the rest of us, that our great victory would be celebrated in Jerusalem, and the populace would rise with us, and the yoke of Roman imperialism would be thrown off once and for all.

Eleazar and I developed a strange relationship, based on mutual mistrust. He promoted me and allowed me to function as one of his lesser commanders because it was in his best interest to do so. He utilized my hero's status for his own purposes, but there was always his piercing gaze that suggested he suspected there was more to me than I had revealed, and, of course, he was right. I was not a circumcised, Torah-abiding Jew, and I was tainted with the blood, the language, and the customs of the enemy. In this camp of zealots, such infirmities could be fatal, if it should ever suit Eleazar's purpose to unmask me. For my part, I was not inclined to accept Eleazar as God's mashiah. The image of him humping the Roman officer was seared into my memory and discouraged the belief that he was God's chosen despite the yearning inside me that wanted to believe.

On the eve of our departure for Jerusalem, Eleazar addressed his greater and lesser troop commanders, including me, as we gathered around a roaring bonfire. Eleazar's spies warned that not all of Jerusalem would be welcoming, especially a former High Priest, Ananus ben Ananus, who seemed to be the power behind the temple aristocracy. We all knew that this sort was sympathetic to the Romans, propped up in their positions of power, prestige, and wealth, and now the spies reported that the priests were asserting their own authority over the city in the power vacuum left behind by the fleeing Romans and their lackey king. What was worse, they were souring the minds of the people over the "unwashed rabble from the Galilee," suggesting that we were merely thieves who would ransack the city.

"We shall beard the lion in his den," Eleazar promised. "We will march straight to the temple, and that is where we shall establish our stronghold."

The stack of bonfire timbers collapsed into itself just then in a cloud of sparks, and a burning log rolled toward Eleazar's feet; he kicked it back into the bonfire.

"Well?" he said in a tone that defied any challenge.

At first there was silence and then came the rhythmic beating of sword against shield, then another, and another until the assembled officers gave their assent to Eleazar's audacious plan in a cacophony of steel against steel.

I was astonished although I timidly joined the sword clanging of the others. The very name "zealot" implied zeal on behalf of God, of rigid obedience to Hebraic law known as Torah, of scrupulous allegiance to the centuries of Hebrew tradition. Even an outsider like me understood that nothing in Hebrew religion was more sacred, nothing in the written words of Torah more central, nothing in Hebrew culture more revered than the temple … the very dwelling place of God; yet, these rebels would profane God's high holy place in order to secure their own power and authority-- not against the Romans but against their fellow Jews who inhabited Jerusalem. Hah! Perhaps Eleazar would choose the innermost sanctum, the holy of holies, for his headquarters. The tactical brilliance of Eleazar's scheme as a military maneuver was exceeded only by its audacity.

As I returned to my tent, my thoughts turned to Jerusalem. I had been there once before. In my thirteenth year, Father and I journeyed to the holy city to make sacrifice at the temple.

"Every man should make this pilgrimage at least once," Father said, "and the year when you are no longer a boy, but a man is the best time."

I remembered the massive white marble walls of the temple that seemed as high as the sky and as brilliant as the midday sun. When we approached, the doorways at the base of the wall opened wide and invited us to enter and climb the ascending flight of stairs that seemed endless. Before entering, father said we should first wash ourselves in a pool, a *miqveh*, so that we would be clean as we came near to God. I humored my father, but I puzzled at his scrupulosity since we paid little heed to Torah ritual in our Damascus synagogue, much less our own home.

What a grand bazaar we encountered when we reached the top of the stairway! Vendors hawked grain, wine, goats, and pigeons for sacrifice, even bulls! Minor priests and Levites in drab, hooded robes regulated the foot traffic and monitored the activities of this outer court of the temple precincts that encircled the inner courts; here was the Court of the Gentiles where even foreigners were permitted.

The courtyard surrounded a magnificent inner tower of gleaming marble and gold. Surely God was inside, and I shielded my eyes as I gazed upon the brilliance that shone brighter than the sun itself. And the height! Much taller than the finest pines or cedars, the top of the tower reached for the heavens.

I was awestruck as a troop of veiled temple dancers passed by on their way to the inner courts, led by a priest in a flat, white turban and flowing purple robes. The entourage included Levite musicians carrying their trumpets, flutes, and lyres. Later, I heard strains of their music seeping from within, and I wished Father had dared enter, but that would have been presumptuous, perhaps unlawful, for Hellenists from Damascus.

Father stepped up to a money changer's booth, and my eyes widened as he counted out ten denarii. Ten! More than a week's wages for my father back in Damascus! I had never seen such an extravagant side of him. With the handful of shekels, we moved along to a vendor of goats, and father picked out two of the finest rams.

With the rams in tow, we sought assistance from a Levite.

"Foreigners are not allowed beyond the Court of Gentiles," he said. "I will wait with you while your sacrifice is offered inside."

A second Levite disappeared with our goat sacrifice, while the first one explained what would happen inside.

"Do you see the smoke rising from the Altar of Burnt Offering?"

We looked where he pointed and watched the smoke curl skyward.

"That is where your sacrifice will be offered. The ram's blood will be sprinkled at the base of the altar, the meat cooked over the open fire, and the entrails burned."

From inside, I heard the plaintive bleating of the goats in their moment of death that signified life.

After what seemed hours, fried goat meat was brought to us. I have never eaten such an important meal. The rest would be eaten or sold by the priests, and the entrails burned into smoke that certainly made a pleasing scent as the tendrils wafted toward the sky. I truly felt holy, and a grown man, as father and I ate our fill.

As I lay on my mat awaiting sleep, I realized that the long-ago day with my father had been a highlight of my life, and I thrilled at the anticipation of my return to the holy city of the descendants of Abraham. Now I would return, not as a pilgrim but as a warrior--or am I a pilgrim still? Perhaps I am a wayfarer on a journey to an uncertain destination that will only be revealed when I arrive.

"Humph!"

I surprised myself and interrupted the snores of the men around me with my audible self-reproach. If there is a purpose to what lies ahead for me, it is beyond my seeing, and I drifted off convinced that I was but a fool seeking meaning where there is none.

As we mustered the following morning, Eleazar asked a priest to read from the sacred scrolls of our people:

I was glad when they said to me, "Let us go to the house of the LORD!" Our feet are standing within your gates, O Jerusalem. Jerusalem—built as a city that is bound firmly together. To it the tribes go up, the tribes of the LORD, as was decreed for Israel, to give thanks to the name of the LORD. For there the thrones for judgment were set up, the thrones of the house of David. Pray for the peace of Jerusalem: "May they prosper who love you. Peace be within your walls, and security within your towers." For the sake of my relatives and friends I will say, "Peace be within you." For the sake of the house of the LORD our God, I will seek your good.

Somehow, I doubted that the coming days would see peace within those holy walls.

Chapter Five

Early-winter rains pelted the brigand army of Eleazar as we journeyed through the Judean hill country. An army moves slowly on its feet and the backs of mules, horses, and oxen. Even at our slow pace, the journey to Jerusalem would be a mere handful of days. The gleaners had long ago left the fields barren, and the shepherds holed up in their lean-tos while the sheep milled about their pens. Well-wishers failed to appear along our path, as we had expected, and high spirits were dampened with each muddy step forward. We were in a foul temper as we pitched our tents in the rain outside the city walls. Our only greeters were beggars at the city gates.

I stripped to my loin cloth and hung up my wet tunic inside the tent when Eleazar's man appeared at the tent flap.

"Come with me, Menachem," he said. "Eleazar summons you."

Me? Why me? Was I discovered? I glanced quickly to check that I was still wearing my loin cloth, and I hastily donned my tunic, not because I was in a hurry to depart with the man, but because I felt the need to cover myself for I suddenly felt naked. I felt the hot glares of the men in my charge as I pulled the damp tunic over my head.

As I entered the tent of our leader, his privy council looked up from their inspection of a drawing on papyrus that I assumed was a sketch of the temple or the city. The tent reeked of damp clothes, unwashed men, and flatulence for the leaders had recently supped on sausages and cheese washed down with barley beer. The only greeting extended by Eleazar was a self-satisfied belch. I detected a slight twitch at the edge of his lips, an inscrutable smile that teased that he knew more about me than I wished. He sat cross-legged on a rug with the sketch laid out before him. Without the pretense of small talk, his gravelly voice matter-of-factly announced that I would be included in the advance party that would attempt to capture the temple yet this night.

"You will be their morale booster," he said as he mocked the mythology of my heroics.

"And, they may need someone who can speak and read Greek well."

There it was. He knew that I was a scribe. Had Rehum betrayed me? What else did Eleazar know? Was he saving the rest for a time when that would suit him? He certainly knew how to use my exalted reputation for valor to his advantage even though I suspected he knew it was all a fantasy. I simply nodded and stood mute as if my speech would reveal all.

With a wave of a thick hand, he dismissed me.

"Get some sleep, if you can," the voice of one his lieutenants followed me out. "Someone will come for you in the dead of night."

I didn't sleep, and I was sitting in the dark on my mat fingering the Roman *gladius* that replaced my flint hunting knife when a gruff voice outside the tent called my name. As I stepped out in the cool night air--the rain had stopped, and the moon shone brightly overhead--I was slapped in the face by a muddy hand.

"Rub this in and spread it around. Your skin shines like a newborn's ass."

I didn't recognize the voice that came from a darkened face, nearly invisible amongst other mud-smeared men, who lingered restlessly in the shadows.

I was near the rear of the group of thirty or so infiltrators as we crept forward in a single line with gaps of one or two paces between us. I was glad of our slow pace; my wound had scabbed over, but pain remained within my knee, and I suspected that the greater injury was under the surface scar. The man who had called to me led the way. As we approached the gate that would be our entrance into the walled city, our leader held up his hand, and we stopped in place and observed. One of the two oil lamps affixed to the wall flickered, but the other was dark. When there is anarchy, no one fills the lamps. There was also a Roman guard station there that appeared empty, of course, since the Romans had fled, but as we drew near, we heard a stirring, and the leader again signaled a stop. He alone stepped toward the booth with his sword held high in a position to strike.

"Alms for the poor. Alms for the poor."

The leader waved us all forward, and the blind beggar who slept in the booth greeted each of us with the same chant.

"Alms for the poor. Alms for the poor."

We regrouped after we had passed through the gate into the city. Although there was a bright moon, the alleyways were dark and quiet as a tomb. We moved forward in twos or threes, stepping quickly through open spaces and then pausing as we pressed against the next wall. I was in the last grouping. As we probed deeper into the city, I sensed we were followed, and my attention turned from the way we were going to the way we had come.

"There, there, did you see it?" I said but the others shrugged it off. I was sure I had seen or heard something, but it was ethereal, a specter, a shadow--something I couldn't quite grasp--but something or somebody was there, I swear.

39

We soon reached the final open space, a plaza with the dark marble walls of the temple looming on the far side. The walls cast a dark shadow over the courtyard. We regrouped again, and the leader whispered,

"On my signal, we shall dash to the far side. Do you see the doorway at the base?" He pointed with his short sword. "That is a gate that leads to a staircase that climbs to the platform inside the temple and the court of the Gentiles. There may be temple police stationed in the stairway."

The brooding dark walls of hewn marble with a speck of an entrance that seemed as tiny as a mole hole appeared impenetrable. How could we squeeze through and mount a charge up the steep steps?

But off we went. It wasn't a long sprint, but it seemed that I was bogged down in a swamp that sucked each step into muck. By the time I ducked into the doorway, the leader had already captured a sleeping guard, and we ascended the steps without incident with the prisoner in tow. The footfalls of our sandals on the hewn-stone steps echoed off the walls and filled the passageway in a rising crescendo as we neared the top.

The staircase opened into a marketplace. The courtyard was covered with stalls for vendors of all sorts, but especially for moneychangers and purveyors of doves, grain, wine, or incense for those pilgrims who didn't bring their own sacrifice but would buy it here. Foreign currency wouldn't do for temple sacrifice, and thus the moneychangers were essential to change foreign coins into Jewish shekels. Many of the vendors slept in their stalls, and the cooing of the doves in their cages seemed incongruent with our mission.

"Here, here, what's this?"

"Be quiet, old man, or you'll feel our steel," our leader gestured with his sword to a vendor who awakened as our prisoner was lashed to a pole that supported an awning over his booth.

The leader assigned further tasks. I was to guard this prisoner and others who would soon arrive. Squads were dispersed to secure the other gates into the temple. A pair returned to the camp outside the city with the news that the temple had been captured and that Eleazar's army could begin to move in.

It was then that the phantom appeared. I didn't see him arrive, but suddenly the blind beggar from the city gate nudged my elbow.

"What ... how ... what are you doing here," I asked.

"I might ask the same of you," he replied.

He was a shrew of a man, who would seemingly be blown away by the slightest breeze. He wore no robe or tunic, only a loincloth and a grimy turban, and his feet were bare. His soiled sheepskin blanket was draped over his shoulders like a cape. He had a beard, of sorts, with a few wisps of white hair trailing behind his turban, and his eyes squeezed tight in a way that said they had never been opened.

Just then, my attention was diverted to a shout on the far side of the plaza that turned out to be nothing.

"Bartimaeus will be watching you," the beggar said, and when I turned back, he was gone. Somehow, I believed him. I believed the blind beggar could sense what others could not. I believed Bartimaeus would keep close watch on the goings-on in the temple and in Jerusalem.

Hours later, the first troops arrived, led by Eleazar himself on his stallion. As the troops came in, the vendors were shooed out. The temple police were released. By late afternoon, the transition was complete, and the courtyard of the Gentiles was filled with the clanging of tent stakes being pounded into the cracks. By nightfall, the plaza had been transformed into an army compound littered with tents. Eleazar and his officers set up their headquarters inside the inner courts, but I'm not sure if Eleazar was brazen enough to enter the holy of holies. It would take a fortnight to transport all the war machines, the ballistae and the catapults, up the steps and to then assemble them, but by year's end, the Jerusalem temple had been transformed into a well-armed fortress.

"We won't see Ananus ben Ananus around here again" Eleazar boasted. "Let the priests set sail for Rome, and we'll see how they are treated by their Roman friends if they no longer have temple plunder to share."

His prediction proved false. Ananus ben Ananus, the former high priest, would rally the city against the usurpers from the Galilee.

Jerusalem 67-68 CE

"I am going to make them eat wormwood and give them poisoned water to drink; for from the prophets of Jerusalem ungodliness has spread throughout the land." Thus, says the LORD of hosts: Do not listen to the words of the prophets who prophesy to you; they are deluding you. They speak visions of their own minds, not from the mouth of the LORD. They keep saying to those who despise the word of the LORD, "It shall be well with you"; and to all who stubbornly follow their own stubborn hearts, they say, "No calamity shall come upon you."

Jeremiah 23:15-17

Chapter Six

Winter passed under a heavy bank of slate-gray clouds. Monotony was the order of the day for Eleazar's encampment on the grounds of the Court of Gentiles. Finally, as spring breezes dried out the tents following the winter rains, Eleazar summoned me again. Although my anxiety always swelled in his presence, I was pleased when he ordered me to lead a delegation seeking an end to the stalemate with the aristocracy. Renewed hope and purpose chased winter's melancholy, at least for the moment.

"Take up your pen and scribe a message to the old fool, Ananus, who thinks he still accounts for something."

The former high priest must still account for something, I thought to myself, if Eleazar feels the need to reach out to him. Ananus had been deposed as high priest a few years earlier, but through dint of intellect and personality, he remained the effective leader of the priests and the aristocracy within the city. Only later, would I learn of the circumstances that led to his prior ouster, which would prove to be of great interest.

I was provided with reed pen, inks, and blank sheets of papyrus on which I would scribe the message to Ananus. I eagerly accepted them and the change in status that the tools of my trade signified. I was again a scribe and no longer a pretender to valor on the battlefield. From that day forward, I carried the familiar implements in my goatskin bag with the reed pen tucked comfortably behind my ear.

The message that I scribed according to Eleazar's instructions encouraged Ananus to join in a coalition that would create a united front to discourage a possible Roman reprisal. Eleazar proposed that he, himself, would be supreme commander of the city and the military forces but that Ananus could fill an ill-defined leadership role--perhaps to be reappointed as high priest--if he would support Eleazar. When I finished, I blew softly on the papyrus sheet to hasten the drying and handed it to Eleazar for a seal. He didn't bother to look it over and simply rolled it into a scroll as I suspected he couldn't read it anyway.

"Take two of your men with you to deliver the message," Eleazar said as he handed the rolled scroll back to me. "Listen closely to their response and report back."

Rehum, my fellow Damascene, had become my principal aide. I relied upon him because I had no alternative, even though I could never be sure that he hadn't divulged my Hellenist background to Eleazar-- somehow, Eleazar had learned that I was a scribe. It helped that Rehum was everything I was not: strong, athletic, and skilled with his weapons. For his part, Rehum assumed the role of my protector, and whether I summoned him or not, he was always near, but I could never be sure whether that was due to loyalty to me or as eyes for Eleazar.

With my delegation, I departed the temple for the first time since our arrival, and I was stunned to see that Jerusalem had become an armed camp. Every man on the street carried a sword, dagger, or cudgel, with wary, darting eyes set in grim faces. Rehum marched at my side with his Roman short sword unsheathed, and he waved it at any who came too near. As powerful as we appeared to ourselves within the temple walls, the forces outside the walls had us encircled, virtual captives within our own stronghold. How eerie it all seemed, especially since we believed we would be welcomed with garlands and singing children, and Jerusalem would become a beacon of unity and hope that would be a light to the nations and discourage the Romans, but Jerusalem hadn't rushed to Eleazar, suspicious of a one-time thief, unwilling to follow a lowly

Galilean, and indignant at his disrespect for the holy temple. Apparently, Ananus and the priests had successfully convinced the people that Eleazar and the zealots were extremists, not to be trusted.

When we reached the hill-top neighborhood comprised of villas of the wealthy, we passed through a barricade manned by guards who interrogated us and searched our bags. When we explained our purpose, we were escorted by half a dozen armed men to the residence of the one-time high priest. We waited a long while on the portico between a pair of magnificent marble columns before a second set of armed guards led us into a rectangular courtyard with rooms on all sides. The fronds atop tall date palms swayed and whispered in the morning breeze. Spring flowers bloomed all around--red roses, yellow daisies, and something delicate and pink that I couldn't identify. A servant offered cracked almonds and dates while we waited. Finally, Ananus ben Ananus and his entourage made their entrance.

The long wait may have been due to the time necessary for Ananus to dress in his priestly attire--to make the proper impression, of course, and I was impressed. An embroidered sash in rich blue, purple, and scarlet bound a body-length, full-sleeve tunic of fine-stitched white linen. Atop his head sat a broad, flat-topped white turban. And the sweet perfume! If such was his casual dress, I wondered at the splendor of the vestments he had worn during ceremonies he conducted as high priest. My comrades and I, with the look of ruffians from the countryside, were at a distinct disadvantage if appearances mattered in such affairs.

We bowed slightly, and I extended the papyrus scroll that contained the message from Eleazar. One of the lesser priests stepped forward to receive the scroll, unrolled it, and read it aloud. The face of Ananus darkened as he listened. His pursed lips quivered as anger visibly rose within him as we waited for his response.

"Bastard!" he spit out.

In a flash of purple indignation, he whirled and stomped out, leaving his assistants to finish the conversation, and they did so with courtesy but firmly pressed their case. It seemed two of them merely conversed with each other as they expressed the view of the aristocrats, and we just listened.

"With all due respect to Eleazar and his military success, Jerusalem should be led by someone the people know and respect, not a Galilean," said the first priest.

"And someone with stature," replied the second.

"Perhaps less extremism and a little moderation would be in order."

"If anyone can negotiate peace with the Romans, it is Ananus."

And so, it went, back and forth.

When we returned to the temple, we reported the gist of the comments to Eleazar, but we omitted Ananus' own single epithet. It didn't matter; Eleazar loosed his own blue streak. From the standpoint of vulgar oaths, our side certainly had the better of it.

My hopes for reconciliation proved short-lived. As the summer sun scorched the stone courtyard and the tent city of the zealots, so too did tensions spike throughout the populace. In a deliberate escalation, Eleazar sent armed troops to arrest the former bureaucrats who had served in the Roman administration. This was a mission for the muscled, and I was happy not to be included.

When the Galilean zealots returned with their captives, bound with cords around their wrists, Eleazar stalked back and forth in front of the prisoners who had the misfortune of working for the former Roman hierarchy as clerks, secretaries, prefects, and other petty administrative positions. These were not the aristocrats of Ananus' crowd but middle-class public servants who turned the wheels of city government. Now, they were deemed traitors to Hebrew interests according to Eleazar. To be sure, there were scoundrels among them who had abused their authority and enriched themselves, but they were the exceptions among the men who now stood accused before Eleazar.

"I protest!" cried one slender man, not yet thirty. "I am merely a clerk with a wife and young children. Jerusalem has been the home of my father, his father, and his father before him. Since the time of King David, Jerusalem has been the cradle for our children; we are of the tribe of Judah; I was circumcised on the eighth day like a proper Jewish man-child; and I tithe and offer appropriate sacrifices in season. I am as loyal as any of you."

The young clerk then spoke directly to Eleazar, who moved to listen, face-to-face.

"Kind Eleazar, you are a magnificent general and a great man, and I pray that you release me to my family."

Eleazar's thick eyebrows twitched as he considered the clerk's plea. After a moment's reflection, he spoke:

"Give me your hands," Eleazar responded, "that I may cut your cords."

Eleazar drew his double-edged *gladius* as the young clerk extended his bound wrists. Eleazar slid the tip of his sword under the cords and sliced them away, but then he grabbed the mop of curly hair atop the man's head with his left hand as he kicked out the clerk's feet, forcing the man to his knees. Raising the sword high, Eleazar chopped down with great force, breaking the young clerk's neck. Blood spackled the other prisoners as Eleazar hacked again and again until he had cut all the way through, and then he held the bloody head high for all to see.

"Who else dares to test my judgment?" Eleazar bellowed.

The decapitated body was thrown into a Jerusalem gutter, but the wide eyes of the severed head stared out over the courtyard for the remainder of the day from atop a tent pole; the next morning, the ravens, whose droppings soiled the gold adornments atop the inner tower, plucked out the eyeballs.

Some of the rebels may have thrilled at this barbarity, but none in my tent. The men ate their mess in silence, if they ate at all, and then a few wandered the courtyard aimlessly while others lay in tight balls on their mats even before the sun's last rays departed the city. Rehum watched me closely; once, I thought he was about to speak, but then his inscrutable face turned away. My knee, which always ached, now throbbed incessantly. I rubbed it for a while, then flexed and extended it, but the pain remained. Finally, I gave up and slumped back on my own mat. Eventually, I must have fallen asleep because I dreamt of bread baking on my mother's hearth under the benign gaze of snow-capped Mt. Hermon.

As summer wound down, Jerusalem sunk toward the morass of civil war. In a desert windstorm, sand dunes appear then disappear and what was there one day was gone the next, and while the dust blows, it is difficult to see the shape of things. So, the shifting alliances would be in

Jerusalem as Eleazar and Ananus competed for support amongst the various factions and sub-factions. For the moment, the armed camps forgot about the Romans, until the first Galilean refugee arrived.

"They burn whole villages and hang the men on crosses," the breathless man reported, with the appearance of one who had run on foot many miles from the Galilee.

Soon other refugees flooded in from the north with reports that, not one but two, Roman legions plus auxiliary cohorts had arrived, led by the hero of prior Roman campaigns, General Vespasian, who had been encouraged out of retirement for the important task of reclaiming Jerusalem. Rome could not allow rebellion in the provinces, and the stain of defeat at Beth Horon must be erased. What was more, there were rumors of a third legion enroute from Alexandria in the south led by General Titus, Vespasian's own son. There would be no ambushes in a valley and nothing to impede tens of thousands of Roman legionnaires from marching upon Jerusalem.

Did anyone truly believe that the Romans would simply turn tail and run? We had been fools; of course, the Romans would retaliate. The giddiness over the victory at Beth Horon was now replaced by the sober reality that the Romans would be back in greater force than before. While the zealots seemed willing, even anxious, to engage in total, apocalyptic warfare, others, led by the former high priest, Ananus ben Ananus, encouraged negotiation and moderation, which seemed like appeasement or treason to the likes of Eleazar.

For myself, I had lost all hope for the cause, and I questioned whether I should stay and fight and certainly die with Jerusalem, or ...? I wasn't yet ready to abandon this holy city but thoughts of retreat to the comfortable life I left behind in Damascus greeted me each day upon awakening and returned as I drifted off at day's end.

Soon, Jerusalem's walls burst with refugees from the countryside seeking sanctuary, and a tent city appeared in the hills around Jerusalem led by another Galilean rebel with battle success against the Romans. The forces under the command of John from the city of Gischala had defended their city from a Roman onslaught, and John claimed that the Romans would be incapable of assaulting the great city of Jerusalem. In a city thirsty for good news, his optimistic promises were gulped down, and Eleazar invited his fellow Galilean general to a parley. With an alliance forged with John, Eleazar hoped Ananus would cede control of all of Jerusalem to Eleazar.

John brought his lieutenants to the temple courtyard, and Eleazar made sure all his officers, including me, were there as a show of force. Eleazar was short and stout, and the Roman *cuirass* he wore barely contained his broad shoulders. John could not boast Roman armor, which made him appear all the thinner by comparison, but the lance he carried seemed an extension of his already impressive length. After John and Eleazar initially strutted about like banty roosters, they soon reached agreement. John of Gischala would prove to be equally as radical as Eleazar--perhaps more so--and his uneasy alliance with Eleazar left Ananus and the voices of moderation with dwindling influence.

All that Jerusalem could do was wait as summer turned into fall into winter. Each day brought more refugees and more news of atrocities by the Romans who seemed in no hurry to advance on Jerusalem itself, content to do mayhem in the countryside. I became totally disgusted with the inability of my fellow Jews to make common cause to prepare for the

51

onslaught to come. Yet, I could see no wisdom on either side. The hardliners invited annihilation with their attitude of fighting to the last man, but when I finally questioned Eleazar's brutality openly, it was nearly the death of me--but, I am getting ahead of myself. Neither could I countenance the appeasing attitude of Ananus and his followers. They were fools to think that a friendly gesture toward the Romans would bring peace, much less prosperity. At this point, even a return to the status quo before the rebellion seemed impossible. I puzzled to make sense of it all, to know God's will in the coming apocalypse.

The monotony of winter was broken up with a new task; twice weekly I led thirty men to the granaries of Malachi the grain merchant. Half the troop pulled barrows brimming with grain back to Eleazar's camp, and the other half guarded our precious cargo. Eleazar's treasury plundered from the Romans at Beth Horon allowed his army to be well-fed even as scarcity plagued the city's populace. With Rehum close at my side, I carried the money purse and the ledgers where I meticulously scribed each transaction.

While returning one late afternoon, the guard at the head of our column stopped suddenly and raised a hand as we entered the plaza outside the temple. Mottled shadows on the temple walls gave the appearance of grime and mold. Many vendor's stalls had long since been abandoned, but commerce continued even in the worst of times, and we paused as another entourage passed through the plaza. At the center of the procession was a priest of high rank according to his vestments and tall turban; lesser priests and bodyguards marched at his side.

When a ruckus broke out nearby, all attention was diverted to the clatter in the crowd, and the priest's bodyguards unsheathed their weapons and stepped forward to shield against any mayhem spilling toward the priest, but it was all a carefully planned diversion. From the rear, a shadow slipped from the crowd. Without hesitation, the assassin plunged a dagger into the back of the holy man, skillfully piercing the heart; only a bewildered grimace on the face of the priest preceded his fall forward, already dead when his face smashed into the cobblestones. Before the bodyguards sensed alarm, the dagger-man assassin melted back into the crowd. The *sicarii* had struck again. Amidst a jumbled clamor of shouts and shrieks, my troop silently marched past. The assassin was our supposed ally, and we were accomplices to the murder of a fellow Jew and holy man.

John of Gischala's *sicarii* targeted leading priests, aristocrats, and other voices of moderation. To John's recent Galilean arrivals, who had witnessed Roman atrocities, any talk of compromise sounded like surrender and any compromiser was deemed to be a Roman sympathizer, worthy of assassination.

The Hebrew blood spilled by the dagger-men only signaled the beginning of civil war.

Again, I was summoned to scribe a letter, and I barely concealed my incredulity at the audacity of the proposed enterprise, a brazen proof that the enemy of my enemy is my friend. My hand shook as I scribed the letter that would be carried to the leaders of Idumea with an invitation to join the battle against the ensconced aristocracy of Jerusalem. The Idumeans from lands to the south were Semitic cousins of the Hebrews, descended from the Edomites rather than one of the twelve tribes of Israel. The Idumeans were marginal followers of Israelite religion, and sometimes their lands were included within the broader Israelite kingdom depending upon the shifting sands of power.

Within a month, we had our answer. Thousands of Idumeans massed at the city gates, and John of Gischala invited them in. Frequent foes of the Jews throughout history, the Idumeans eagerly joined in common cause with the peasants from the Galilee, and centuries of repressed anger against the Jerusalem leadership resulted in blood-swollen gutters.

From inside the temple walls, I listened with horror as screams of the dying filled the night. Each shriek was my own. Was this the good and noble cause I had joined? I was distraught and entirely disillusioned. It seemed that even the most well-intentioned efforts of humankind were illusory, vainglorious, and feeble, at best, or depraved, at worst. If I had previously worried that my life, indeed all of life, was empty, meaningless, and without value, now I was convinced. If these marble walls had come tumbling down on top of me, I would not have been more crushed in spirit than the pitiable state in which I found myself. I had come seeking the reign of God, but from the very first, I had been slipping deeper and deeper into despair, and now I had fallen off the cliff altogether, and I floated in nothingness. Perhaps it had been release from the captivity of life into the freedom of death that had been in the eyes of the Roman *aquilifer*. Though I lacked the will to live, I also lacked the courage to die, and so I went on living simply because I was too weak in spirit to do otherwise.

It seemed that Eleazar now only appeared while astride, as if he required the separation and the elevation to relate to his troops and to the mayhem they did at his bidding. Or, perhaps he simply avoided the piles of stinking garbage that accumulated in all corners of the courtyard. When Eleazar assembled his troops one day to flag sagging spirits with the news

54

of a "victory," I listened with humor, for the grotesque had become laughable.

"These three, our friends from Idumea, have performed a great service," Eleazar intoned as he sat high upon his stallion.

Three Idumean henchmen stood alongside his horse with sheepish grins, not quite comfortable in these surroundings or perhaps the light of day. Eleazar described how the three had cut the throats of the guards at the villa of Ananus ben Ananus during the dead of night before they crept into the former high priest's bed chambers and stabbed him where he slept.

"And so, this wolf in sheep's clothing, this Roman-loving deceiver, this enemy of the people has met his just reward," Eleazar said, and the mob dutifully cheered.

I laughed inwardly. When the Romans arrived, they would find a city filled with corpses, except for Eleazar ben Simon and John of Gischala who would be engaged in swordplay, each covered with wounds and bleeding profusely but alive in eternal combat.

God's reign on earth didn't come to pass that year. Amidst the chaos, shifting alliances, and assassinations, I wondered whether such a thing was even possible--at least not without destroying it all and starting anew.

Perhaps that's what God intended.

Chapter Seven

Damp straw reeking of horse piss blanketed me and two others from Damascus as we lay hidden in a Jerusalem stable. When the shouts in the street drew near, the snorts and whinnies of the geldings muffled our breaths. As the hours passed, it seemed that my entire life had been spent writhing in horse manure. The stench of the stable became my own.

After the sun set in the Judean hills, dancing torches lit up the alleyway outside the stable. Through a crack in the wallboards, shadows flickered against the brick and mortar of the far wall, and I imagined the contorted face of my poor wife, dead in childbirth. When I shut my eyes, her smile washed over me. Would I soon join her? I expected so, and I neither feared death nor welcomed it. I was merely numb.

When the vacant eyes of the Roman *aquilifer* whose life I had taken stared at me again, as they did so often in that murky place between wake and sleep, I believed I saw what he saw in his moment of death: folly and futility. Two years ago, I had joined this cause that I now rejected, and which was on the verge of claiming me as just another victim. I no longer felt guilt over taking the man's life for we were now bonded in eternal sameness. I was him, and he was me. We were merely chaff tossed by a capricious breeze.

For months I had known that my time with Eleazar's army would be limited. When the order went out that all Gentiles should be purged from Jerusalem, I knew that the day would soon arrive. I had always known it would come down to this and that my lack of circumcision would be my doom. What I didn't know was that two dear friends from Damascus, brothers Rufus and Alexander, would share my fate.

Earlier that day as the sun beat down from on high, Eleazar pranced about on his stallion, overseeing the inspection and execution. Suspected Gentiles had been arrested and brought to the temple where they were lined up along the wall. I watched as zealots ripped off robes and tunics to check for the distinguishing mark of the Jewish male; the circumcised were dismissed and allowed to exit the temple grounds, but Gentiles were dispatched with a quick flick of a hooked dagger that sliced off far more than the uncircumcised tips of the Gentile men, who soon bled out leaving scores of corpses in a vast pool of crimson.

It was then that I spotted Rufus and Alexander. What were they doing here in Jerusalem? I had grown up with the brothers, and our parents had been mainstays of the Damascus synagogue that followed Iesou of Nazareth. Were they circumcised or not? Would they pass the hideous test or not? I didn't know. Circumcision within our synagogue was not critical and some were circumcised, but others were not. As the zealot bullies pushed them toward the wall, I stepped forward and protested to Eleazar.

"I know those two," I said as I pointed out the brothers. "I grew up with them in Damascus, and I will vouch for them."

For a moment, Eleazar hesitated. His stallion was restless and chafed at the bit, tossing his head and snorting. Eleazar jerked hard on the reins, and the stallion stepped back. Then the moment I had long anticipated came to pass.

"Well then, Menachem, or should I say "Markos," step over with them, and you shall all be tested."

"My general, I have fought for you, I have killed for you, and I have been your faithful servant. Please stop this madness. This cannot be the will of God."

The would-be mashiah had set his course, and there could be no reversal. To relent would be to show weakness; to reconsider would be to acknowledge error; to forgive would be to condemn himself. I had grown to despise the man, but a strange pity washed over me as I realized the poor soul was frightened. Eleazar was afraid of himself, afraid that he had chosen the wrong path, and afraid that his vision, his understanding, his sense of the will of God had been misguided, but for a fanatic, there can be no turning back, and Eleazar became more tenacious, zealous, and resolute and his cruelty only heightened as if to prove himself honorable and righteous and hold his self-doubt at bay.

"Step forward or I shall lop off your head myself," Eleazar said.

Numbly, I joined my friends at the wall. The dagger would soon slice away my manhood, and my lifeblood would splash over the cut stones of the Temple as a sacrifice to this false mashiah. I sucked in a deep breath and held it. My knees weakened even as I prayed for the strength to stand.

Just as the dagger man stepped toward me, my third friend from Damascus, Rehum--the fully circumcised Jew from a Torah-abiding synagogue--emerged from the rabble. In a moment that seemed a lifetime, Rehum grabbed a broken pole from a moneychanger's booth, and he cracked the dagger man across the back of his head, sending the hooked blade slowly tumbling in the air, glistening in the white sunlight, finally clattering on the stones.

"Run, friend," said Rehum, pushing me ahead.

Amidst the wails of the dying, three men from Damascus sprinted toward the mole-hole gate in the temple wall as Rehum, the fourth Damascene, and perhaps the only Torah-pure Jew among us, stood his ground to cover our escape. I never saw him fall, but his defense of me was surely his suicide.

Rufus and Alexander disappeared into the gate ahead of me, but I lagged, slowed by my maimed knee. Just before I arrived at the head of the stairs, the clop, clop of the stallion's hooves on the cut-stone plaza pounded at my heels. The snout of the charging beast knocked me sprawling on the stones just as Eleazar's sword whistled past my head. I crabbed my way into the narrow gate behind my friends who were ahead of me, and we stumbled down the staircase to the streets of Jerusalem. Rufus and Alexander led the way through winding streets and back alleys to a stable, and the stable master covered us with stinking straw until the moonless night would cover our escape.

After a full day and half the night spent cowering in the stable's stink, darkness fell over us as the street quieted and the crackling torches dimmed. My eyes strained to pierce the darkness, but I could see only the outline of the massive neck of the gelding above me, haltered to an iron ring in the oaken wall. More hours passed in the still night. Soon it would be cockcrow.

There were occasional shrieks in the distance, and wailing, and once I was sure I heard weeping from inside the stable. Was it Rufus? Alexander? Had the cry come from deep in my own breast? A bawling baby on the street? I choked and sat bolt upright in a fit of coughing; when quiet returned, I laid down again.

My entire existence had been reduced to a whimpering clump of horse dung. Lying in the squalor of the stable, I finally surrendered to the pain low in my gut. I loosed my bladder and soiled myself. What did it matter? I slept in snatches, but a recurring dream of dagger-wielding Galileans slashing at me awakened me each time, searing the image of Eleazar's hideous grin into my waking consciousness.

The whinny of the gelding that towered over me signaled the return of the stable master. The time was right to make our escape.

"Follow me," the stable master said.

I searched the eyes of my fellows who now seemed as strangers to me: ashen faces, hollow eye sockets, stooped and gaunt with robes caked in manure. The stable master handed each of us a shiny blade. Roman short swords. The bony grip fit well into my palm. I wanted to drop the *gladius*, but I could not, I had become a man of violence, but who was my enemy? I folded the weapon into my robes and followed the others as we slipped into the dawn's early glimmers, stepping from one shadow to the next.

When I stumbled and fell over a lifeless body, I stared into the bulging eyes of the dead man who seemed to be the *aquilifer* from the battle at Beth-Horon, and I tried to shake the stiff body to life, but the face remained contorted in the grimace of the terrible moment of his death.

Breathing heavily, I clambered to my feet, but I had lost sight of the others. When I followed the lane to the right, a patchy-haired mutt growled and bared his teeth, and I retreated. I moved in the direction of muffled voices only to come face-to-face with strangers as frightened as I was. I instinctively raised my sword, but when the strangers gasped and cowered under the expected blow, I dropped the *gladius*, and the clanging steel on the cobblestones seemed an alarm that echoed through the alleyways loud enough to wake the dead.

"Come fool. Come this way."

I followed the whispered voice of the stable master around one corner and then another in the maze of narrow streets. The pale dawn filtered through the silhouettes of two-storey buildings. He hesitated at a thick wooden door, glancing left and right as he pushed the door open, and we joined a throng of huddled, faceless souls.

When a child whimpered, a young mother clasped her palm over his trembling lips and soothed his fears with a kiss on his forehead. I was oddly captivated by the woman whose gentle gaze calmed me, and I sensed we had arrived at a safe oasis amid a desert storm.

The stable master tugged at my robe, and we elbowed our way to where Rufus and Alexander waited.

"We are among friends," the stable master said. "We are gathered here with the followers of Yeshua. This was the home of Ya'akov, the recently-murdered brother of Yeshua and former leader of the Nazarenes. It is now the home of his granddaughter, Anina."

I spun around to look for the woman who exuded tranquility, but the next of kin of Iesou of Nazareth had left the room.

Chapter Eight

The bright morning sun seared my eyelids, and I awoke with a start. Had I been dreaming? Had the temple ordeal been real? I was confused in a strange place with strangers arguing with flailing arms but muted voices. Next to me, Rufus and Alexander leaned against a half-height wall, straining to catch snatches of the animated conversation.

After a few cleansing breaths, I remembered that we had climbed the stairs to the flat roof of the single-storey house of Anina, but then it had been dark, and now it was full daylight. A thatched roof extended over a portion of the expanse, and a solid oak table and chairs rested under cover of the thatch where the jabbering men clustered. Occasionally, one would peel away from the group to furtively scan the streets below, but only ghosts and rumors travelled the empty lanes.

I guessed that the men huddled around the table were the twelve, the Nazarene leadership council. God was mischievous. We were Hellenists from Damascus who escaped annihilation only to fall under the protection of the Nazarenes who once failed to provide sanctuary for another Hellenist, Stephen the martyr.

The Nazarenes were the Torah-abiding followers of Yeshua that included Cephas, also called Petros, and the original disciples of Iesou who continued in Jerusalem after the crucifixion. The home of Ya'akov, the brother of Yeshua, had become their headquarters and Ya'akov their leader, and that is where we now found ourselves.

The Hellenistic Jews of Stephen's circle founded the Damascus congregation after they had been hounded out of Jerusalem following the stoning of Stephen. Stephen dared to criticize the Hebrew hallmarks-- Torah and temple--and the twelve stood with the Pharisees and not with

Stephen when he had been arrested, tried, and executed. The Greek-speaking Hellenists didn't always eat the right foods, not all were circumcised, and we seemed more Gentile than Jew to Hebrew purists, including the Torah-abiding followers of Yeshua led by Ya'akov, his own brother. My distrust of the haughty Nazarenes came naturally, but now my life depended upon their hospitality.

My father had been one of those Hellenists who fled Jerusalem. Simon of Cyrene, the father of Rufus and Alexander, was another. My Gentile mother had long been the leader of the Damascus congregation, and I grew up filling the common chalice with wine, lighting candles, and scurrying about underfoot--and hearing stories in which these Nazarenes had been vilified, and now they were my protectors.

I crabbed on hands and knees over to the brothers, Rufus and Alexander. Even in their reclining position, their height was obvious. Tall and thin as the trunk of a palm tree, the two were clearly brothers with long, pointy noses under wide-set eyes like saucers and olive-skin stretched tight over long faces.

I spread my hands with palms up and whispered, "What are you doing here?"

"We were on business in the Galilee, and we were caught up in the Roman advance," Rufus whispered back.

The brothers were in the warehouse business in Damascus. Damascus was at the crossroads of the caravan trails, and the brothers were trans-shippers.

"I never wanted to leave Damascus," Alexander claimed. "I knew it would be dangerous."

"No, it was your idea to personally deliver a shipment of spices to Capernaum. I was the one who was reluctant to leave Damascus," Rufus replied.

I stifled a smile, the first in months. The argumentative brothers remained as I fondly remembered them. For an instant, we were again urchins on the Damascus streets, swiping apples from an unsuspecting vendor in the market, but stern Simon, their father, marched us back. "It was Alexander's idea," Rufus pleaded, but his brother shot back, "You grabbed two, and I only grabbed one."

Just then, a dove perched atop the peak of the thatched roof. As I watched the gray bird bob its head and strut about, it occurred to me that I hadn't noticed any birds in months. With my head raised skyward, I also noticed wispy, white clouds against a deep blue sky. Holed up in the temple courtyard, I felt the heat of the blazing sun, but now the azure sky was cool and soothing.

"Since our return to Damascus was blocked, we sought refuge in Jerusalem with the other refugees, and we found our way here to the Nazarene followers of Iesou," Alexander's words returned me to the discussion. "When we tried to leave the city by way of the Jericho road to the east, the Idumeans arrested us and turned us over to the zealots."

"And what are you doing here," Rufus asked in a tone both quizzical and accusing.

I shrugged and smiled weakly. "It's a very long story. One day, I'll share it with you. For the moment, please call me "Menachem".

Rufus and Alexander stared at each other with wrinkled foreheads and knit eyebrows, like looking in a mirror, and together they mouthed the name, "Menachem."

Just then, we became the focus of attention of the twelve.

"Were you in the temple? What happened?"

The question was directed to me, and I said we had been captives of the zealots but escaped.

A tall man canted his head, raised his eyebrows, and peered at me. "Why were you arrested? Why did you flee? Why was your life in danger?"

The accusing tone chilled me, but before I was forced to acknowledge my lack of circumcision, the young mother and child ascended the stairway. The elders stood and bowed, and the woman kissed the tall man, the apparent leader with the stern manner. She was a sturdy woman, but she moved with elegance. Curly auburn locks peeked from under her headscarf, and the chubby youngster who followed with one hand clutching her robe had the hair and round face of his mother. After whispering a few words to the leader, she moved toward the three of us from Damascus and bowed slightly as she greeted us.

"I am Anina," she said. "Welcome to my home." She gestured toward the tall man with a wave of her hand. "That is Mishael, my husband, and this young man is Mattithyahu, our son."

The husband glanced toward us and acknowledged our presence with a barely audible grunt before quickly turning back to the men surrounding the oak table, and the murmuring swelled again. For the moment, the Nazarenes forgot us.

"I regret we cannot offer you proper hospitality," Anina said as her son buried his face in her robe, "but we have only a few small loaves from yesterday's baking and water enough to slake your thirst." Then she added, after her nose caught a whiff of our stench, "Perhaps we can spare a pitcher or two for bathing. Come Mattithyahu. Let us bring food and water to these men."

With that, the young woman disappeared down the steps, but she reappeared momentarily with a plate of dried figs, small loaves of flatbread, and another woman carried a pitcher of water and a basin.

"Pardon my husband," Anina whispered, "but he is distracted by the catastrophe that has befallen Jerusalem. The yoke of leadership weighs heavily on his shoulders and those of my cousin, Symeon, who was chosen to succeed my grandfather as our leader."

I had many questions, but this was not the time. Here was the granddaughter to Ya'akov and the grandniece of Yeshua, but she had more pressing worries than to engage in idle chatter with filthy fugitives from Damascus. There was a glowing nobility about her, which should have been odd in these surroundings, but it was not, and the others treated her with warm respect. She was their princess, the closest living relative of Yeshua in this clan of his followers; many were the immediate kin of those who had been his associates. In the days to follow, I would learn that the subtle strength of her own personality also accounted for her high regard.

When it was my turn to wash, Rehum's inscrutable visage smiled at me from the water in the basin. Perhaps I should have felt guilty at Rehum's sacrifice, at least for doubting him, but instead I was simply bewildered--and perhaps a bit embarrassed. Certainly, I looked at him differently, but at myself as well. New questions had been added to my puzzlement. Why had I come? Why had I stayed? Why had Rehum sacrificed his own life to save mine?

I swirled my hand in the water to dispel the image, and my own blanched face appeared. My normally ruddy cheeks over a patchy beard were drained of life. So too my eyes: colorless, vacant, and wary. My prominent cheekbones had taken over my face that now seemed that of a skeleton. Except for the reddish tinges in my hair that I had inherited from my Gentile mother, I was so non-descript as to be a non-person. My skull cap was missing, probably buried in horse manure back at the stable along with the reed pen that was gone from behind my ear; my goatskin bag with my inks and papyri was also gone.

To my surprise, Anina herself dipped the sponge into the basin and began to wipe my face. As droplets of water dribbled through my beard onto my smelly robes, it seemed that more than grime was washed away. For the moment, at least, I was neither fearful, nor despairing, nor hopeless. There was an unseen aura about the woman that I could only sense, and her touch soothed me. Despite the storm of civil war that raged on all sides, I felt sanctuary.

"What is your name," she asked as she rose to her feet to leave.

"Mar ... Menachem."

I lied, and she knew it. At first, she didn't respond as she dried her hands on her apron. I almost blurted out the truth, but I wasn't that brave. She carried the basin of soiled water to the edge of the rooftop. After surveying the alleyway, she splashed the water on the dusty stones below.

"Comforter," She said when she returned to me.

She must have seen a look of puzzlement on my face.

"Comforter," she repeated with a grin tugging at the corners of her mouth. "Don't you know the meaning of your own name? 'Menachem' means 'comforter.'"

She took a step or two toward the stairway, but then turned back. She reached out and placed her hand on my head, squeezed her eyes shut, and whispered a prayer, "for Menachem, the comforter."

Sitting here on the rooftop among the Nazarenes jarred preconceptions from my upbringing. Anina's grace belied the Damascus storyline that the Nazarenes were haughty, self-righteous Hebrew purists who rejected Gentiles as unclean and unworthy followers of the slain mashiah, but more than anything, Anina's curly locks, her slightly portly stature, and her persistent smile under penetrating eyes did not fit with the ethereal Iesou—distant and otherworldly--proclaimed in my Damascus congregation. The touch of her hand was soft and warm. She was flesh and blood and bone, kin of the man she called Yeshua.

Perhaps I was a bit perturbed as well. She ignored my stench and my lie, and instead of validating my well-earned shame, she merely smiled and teased me--nay, it was more than that, she challenged me--with the meaning behind my ill-chosen name. If the name was a falsity, so too must be its meaning.

After Anina disappeared down the steps, the animated debate of the twelve brought me back. The Nazarenes had enemies aplenty, but few allies. Angry voices proclaimed a pox on the Herodians, a pox on the priests, a pox on the Sadducee aristocrats, a pox on the false mashiah and his zealots, and a pox on the Romans. I heard vengeful words; it had been Ananus ben Ananus who ordered the execution of Ya'akov, a handful of years earlier. What was more, I learned, Ananus' actions in arresting and executing Ya'akov had been the reason the High Priest had been deposed. Understandably, no tears had been shed in this household when news of the assassination of Ananus flashed through the streets of Jerusalem. I heard militant words; the Romans were on the run and now was the time to press the attack. I heard words of realism; the Romans lifted a heavy hammer, and when the legions swung with full force, Jerusalem would be smashed. Mostly, I heard words of patience; Yeshua was the mashiah, not Eleazar, not John of Gischala, nor this one or that one, and the Nazarenes would await Yeshua's return to smite the Romans, but what to do in the meantime?

I was uncomfortable at the lack of a plan. Mishael seemed earnest enough, but he merely repeated threadbare platitudes--"Yeshua will return." If the mashiah was truly going to lead the legions of God, now seemed a good time. I had believed in the righteous cause, but look where that had brought us, and I don't think it was merely because I had trusted the wrong mashiah. I think we simply misunderstood.

A fortnight passed. Nazarene men came and went from the former home of Ya'akov, including his cousin Symeon, the co-leader along with Mishael. Symeon was older than the rest of the twelve. A heavyset man with a thundering voice and commanding manner, I wondered if he was anything like his cousin, the crucified Yeshua. When Symeon appeared to take charge, Mishael seemed glad to retreat to the background.

The three of us from Damascus made ourselves useful by venturing into the streets to gather food and water. The streets were mostly empty in an uneasy calm; for the moment, the killing had abated. I drew water from a nearby rectangular pool, and several times when I knelt to fill water skins and jars, I thought I saw an image reflected on the sheen of the water, but when I looked up--nothing. I was sure I was watched by a furtive specter whose sympathies were a mystery.

I returned to the granaries of Malachi.

"Hah! I thought you were dead," he said.

The grain merchant played no favorites, and he accepted the shekels of the Nazarenes as readily as he filled the barrows of Eleazar.

For the right price, figs and dates could be found, but there was no mutton or fish. With each passing day, the prices rose higher as scarcity mounted. There seemed to be no point beyond daily survival. There was no future, only a miserable present. Floating over all was the nagging question: where was God in all this?

Indecision ended the day that leaders of the sect of the Pharisees came to visit.

Between the Roman-leaning aristocrats on the one hand and the zealots on the other, the Pharisees ploughed the middle ground. Ya'akov had been a Pharisee and so was Mishael, the husband of Anina. If the Nazarenes were to find allies, it would be the Pharisees.

The leader of the Pharisees, Yochanan ben Zaccai, led his entourage up the steps to the second-story verandah of the house of Ya'akov. When he reached the top, he immediately sat himself down in the big oaken chair at the head of the table. With both hands, he took hold of the goblet of water set before him and drank deeply before he surveyed his audience, pausing to make eye contact with each one. War-torn Jerusalem had not dulled the luster in his eyes.

"I have been here before, you know," he said. "Under this very roof I broke bread and drank wine with Ya'akov. I was among his Pharisee friends who implored the governor to punish Ananus ben Ananus who ordered his murder a handful of years ago. At least, the governor deposed the criminal," the Pharisee leader said as he looked down, shook his head, and made a series of clucking sounds with his tongue.

Lifting his face again, he said, "We must remember our friends in these desperate times. They are certainly not the motley mix of fools, murderers, and half-breed Idumeans brought in to sow destruction."

"We intend to plead for peace," he said as his gaze again captured each listener in turn. "The Romans will return, and not with five thousand as before but with ten times as many or more. Already, General Vespasian is laying waste to the villages of the Galilee."

"What say you?" The man's eyes flashed steel as he implored the Nazarenes to stand with the Pharisees.

Uncomfortable silence followed, a buzzing fly the only sound. Finally, Symeon, the cousin of the brothers, Yeshua and Ya'akov, who became the leader of the Nazarenes upon the death of Ya'akov, grunted to clear his throat, and his deep voice seemed loud even when he spoke softly.

"You speak with great wisdom, Rabbi Yochanan. We also see no hope of resisting the Romans. Neither Eleazar ben Simon nor any other is the mashiah. We will trust in our Lord, Yeshua of Nazareth, and we await the day when he returns. Only then will Israel be set free."

The visage of Rabbi Yochanan darkened briefly, and his lips quivered, but no sound came from his throat. For nearly four decades, he had listened to the silliness of the Nazarenes. *Yeshua is alive, and he will soon return.* A harmless boast, standing alone, but the harm would come if the Nazarenes chose reliance on a phantasm instead of common sense. He gathered himself before responding.

"Yes, yes. Trust as you will. If that day comes, and your mashiah returns, we will all rejoice, even if we presently have our doubts about your crucified mashiah. While we await the glorious future, we must live in the present. Will you join us in our peace entreaties to General Vespasian and the Roman legions?"

The rabbi spoke delicately, but his words pricked festering Nazarene frustration and embarrassment. Yeshua had not returned, and the Nazarenes had grown weary of defending a promise that had soured with each passing year, and their ranks had declined as the fire of the first days became a smoldering ember. Now, the survival of their very movement and the promises of Yeshua were threatened.

Symeon responded with a hard edge.

"Perhaps this present danger arises because of hard hearts. Perhaps the crucified one has not yet returned because of unbelief. Perhaps this generation is ashamed of the truth."

One of the rabbi's entourage pounded the floor with his staff and others raised fists and hooted, but Rabbi Yochanan held up his hands, and the growling stopped before it escalated. The rabbi inhaled a deep breath and slowly exhaled. He dropped his hands and purposefully placed both palms on the table.

"Now is not the time for recriminations," he said. He lifted his face and stared into the eyes of Symeon. "It is a simple question. Will you stand with us?"

Symeon shifted uneasily on his feet. "We wish you well and will offer prayers of support for your mission to the Romans, but if you fail, then what? Will you stand and fight?" Symeon's question hung in the air as the buzzing fly sought a landing place.

From the back, Mishael broke the silence. "The Nazarenes will not take up arms," he said softly, and his voice wavered. "This is not our war, this is not our mashiah, and this is not our time."

Symeon glanced at the Nazarene leaders. He saw subtle nods, encouraging him to speak freely and reveal the plans of the Nazarenes to their Pharisee friends.

"Our community will soon flee from Jerusalem," Symeon announced.

Rabbi Yochanan's mouth dropped, and he stammered, "y, you, you will abandon mother Jerusalem?"

Chapter Nine

If we were to flee, we needed a plan. Symeon dispatched Rufus, Alexander, and me to reconnoiter a gate exiting the city to seek a safe escape route; other scouts would check other gates. We departed the home of Ya'akov during the still of the night. Ash from the hearth had been mixed with olive oil and smeared over our faces and exposed skin, and we wore the darkest robes to be found.

"Let us follow this lane," Alexander said.

"No, that one only twists around and leads nowhere," Rufus replied.

We settled on a third route, an alleyway. Slipping from one shadow to the next, we pressed our backs against the walls of the buildings we passed. The brothers seemed entirely at ease as we sidled along, but each beat of my heart seemed a shout in the dark.

As we neared a gate on the eastern edge of the city, overlooking the valley of the River Kidron, muted voices told us the gate was guarded. From our vantage on the street, there was little to see without exposing ourselves, but Rufus pointed up at the flat roof of a building. The brothers laced their fingers together and gestured for me to climb up; they lifted me high enough that I could grasp the edge of the roof, and they pushed, and I pulled myself the rest of the way.

Once on the roof, I laid on my back and gazed at the night sky as I caught my breath and calmed myself by counting stars. My bones were weary, and I wished for sleep. When I awoke, I would be in Damascus, and my mother would feed me a bowl of rice and steaming lamb stew. How many times had the moon waxed and waned since I first joined Eleazar's army? I couldn't remember. Too many. I longed for home.

"Psst! Psst! What are you doing up there? What do you see?"

74

I exhaled a deep sigh and rolled over onto my belly. Like a lizard in the desert, I crawled forward to see what I could see.

Symeon would not like my report. The rumors were true. Clusters of Idumeans in twos and threes milled about the gate. Even worse, just outside the gate, many tents were illumined by Idumean camp fires. Whether the legend of Jacob stealing the birthright from his brother Esau was true or not, Idumean folklore remembered the affront to Esau, their legendary forbearer, and spilling the blood of any descendant of Jacob was appropriate justice in Idumean eyes. All Jews were fair targets for the slaughtering Idumeans and moving the mass of Nazarenes through this gate would be impossible.

Just then, a baby cried, and soon a lamp flared inside the building across the alley. A dim light spilled through a window onto the street where the brother's waited; they were in plain view, and they ducked into the shadows.

Rufus whispered as loudly as he dared, "You must drop to the street and come up running."

I could not. I convulsed in sobs. The tears of the child stirred up deep currents. My Damascus grief had been submerged under the stormy seas of Beth Horon and Jerusalem but now burst through the surface in wave after blubbering wave.

"Stay! Stay up there!" Alexander said. "Idumeans come this way!"

Rufus and Alexander disappeared down an alleyway, but I was stuck atop this rooftop. The danger of the moment quelled my tears, and I barely breathed as gruff talk filled the street below. Minutes passed. Then an hour. Then I heard the cock crow.

As deftly as I could manage, I lowered myself while grasping the roof edge, and then I dropped. When my feet struck the cobblestones, I crumpled in a clumsy heap, and my scarred knee screamed. I scrambled to my feet and hobbled into the shadows. The Idumean guards didn't notice, and I returned to Anina's home safely.

All the scouts offered similar reports. Every gate to the city was crawling with Idumeans at all hours of day and night. The Nazarenes' hope to depart was blocked, and I returned to the frustration of inaction, but my consolation was the opportunity for conversation with Anina. After I returned with wheat one day from Malachi's granary, I joined her in the small walled-in space behind the house where she baked flat loaves daily.

"I see a deep sadness in your eyes," Anina said to me. "What is your great hurt?"

"Sadness? Yes, I suppose so," I shrugged my shoulders. "Disillusionment is maybe a better word. And doubt. Disillusionment and doubt."

Her forehead wrinkled, and her eyes narrowed as her gaze seemed to bore into my own eyes. After a few breaths and a slight nod, she spoke again.

"Yes, these are dispiriting times, but you didn't answer my question. What is the pain in your heart that brings weeping to your eyes, that slumps your shoulders, and curls your mouth into a frown?"

I looked away and stared blankly at the clouds as if I searched for an answer there. Without looking at her, I responded.

"A friend whom I doubted saved my life by sacrificing his own."

I lied. Oh, it was true enough that Rehum saved my life in exchange for his own, but I mentioned him as a diversion. I wasn't prepared to speak with Anina about Damascus. Why not? Did I not trust her? No, the better answer is that I did not trust myself following the blubbering pool I became at the mere sound of a crying babe. Nor was I willing, or able, to gaze again into the vortex that had whirled around me on the Damascus rooftop, sucking up love, hope, meaning, and purpose. I ran away then, and I was running still.

"Of course, you should grieve your friend," she replied, "but is it not a good thing that he saw something in you that was worth laying down his own life?"

What? She put a spin on Rehum's death that I hadn't seen, and this conversation was heading down a rat hole. I was quickly learning that Anina could have that effect. Oddly, I hadn't felt guilty about his death. If anything, I felt guilty only because I didn't feel guilty. Instead, I had been confused, perhaps even embarrassed, at his nonsensical sacrifice, but I dismissed his irrational act as just another foolish gesture in a meaningless world. Now, Anina suggested Rehum had not been a fool. Even more unnerving, she subtly challenged me to find a purpose worthy of his sacrifice.

Neither of us spoke for a few moments, but then she pulled on my sleeve, compelling me to gaze into her face.

"What was the goodness that he saw in you?"

God only knows.

I continued with my daily task of fetching grain and water, but I could sense that I was under scrutiny. Whenever I drew water from the pool, I felt the presence of another, but when I cast wary eyes about, I never saw anything.

77

Then came the day that the specter appeared. As I leaned over the water, a beggar tugged at my robe.

"Away with you," I said. "I have nothing for you."

"I want nothing *from* you," the shrew of a man said, "but I have something *for* you. I can lead you safely beyond the walls of Jerusalem."

I turned to find blind Bartimaeus, the phantom who followed us that first night when we captured the temple. I sucked in a deep breath as his offer sifted through my thoughts. Despite the absurdity of his claim, I couldn't resist delivering the man to the twelve. I led Bartimaeus up the stairs to the rooftop verandah and presented him to Symeon, Mishael, and the others. A large goblet was filled with red wine and placed before the blind man as he assumed the place of honor at table's head.

"Even the blind and the lame will turn you back," the man mumbled. He drained the goblet and held it up as if to ask for more. When it was refilled, he said again, "Even the blind and the lame will turn you back."

"He's a drunkard and a fool," came a voice from the rear. "Throw him out to the dogs."

Murmurs swelled, but Anina's husband Mishael, the Pharisee who had studied the holy scrolls of old, held up his hand.

"I know those words," he said. "I have heard those words before."

The blind man repeated them again, more loudly than before. "Even the blind and the lame will turn you back."

He raised his empty goblet again, and Mishael quickly filled it. The blind man's riddle captured Mishael, and he wanted to hear more. Bartimaeus lifted his face and stared with unopened eyes at the men who surrounded him as if he saw them. His mouth opened in a broad, toothless grin.

"How did King David capture Jerusalem from the Jebusites?" he asked with the sense that he knew even if they did not. "Where David came in, the followers of the son of David can go out."

"That's it!" Mishael said. "Anina, where are your grandfather's scrolls of old?"

Mishael and Anina scrambled down the stairs as the men jabbered. Blind Bartimaeus was ignored for the moment, but he didn't seem to mind as he listened to the animated prattle with a self-satisfied smirk, sipping this cup of wine more slowly than the first two. Within minutes, Mishael reappeared with a scroll in his hand. He was breathless as he read aloud the account of David's conquest of Jerusalem a thousand years earlier by infiltrating the city through a water shaft. The story from the scroll included the line, "Even the blind and the lame will turn you back." When he finished, all eyes turned to the blind beggar who offered hope.

"It is true," Bartimaeus said. "Jerusalem sits atop a honeycomb of caves, tunnels, and underground streams. The blind will lead you out."

Chapter Ten

"It's absurd," Symeon snarled, "the blind leading us through a maze."

The upturned lips at the corner of his mouth said that he merely stated a self-evident truth. Several of the twelve grunted their agreement and others nodded.

I could stand it no longer. For days, I had listened from the edge to the meek do-nothings with no plan other than to wait for heavenly intervention, but when I attempted to speak, the words stuck in my throat. My barely audible squeak surprised me as well as the others, and my courage nearly deserted me when all eyes glared at me.

"I'll go," I started again after clearing my throat. "Send me with Bartimaeus as a test. If he speaks the truth, I'll return to gather the rest of you."

"If you get out, why wouldn't you run back to Damascus?" asked Symeon.

"So, you concede the absurdity as a possibility," I said.

I was surprised at my own cussedness, but my confidence was rising. If anything, the wide-eyed, black scowl from Symeon added to my assurance.

It was after the middle of the night when I arrived at the pool, a popular source of water for the city and the same pool that I visited to replenish the water supply in Anina's house. The pool was a rectangular man-made structure of stone and mortar. There was nothing secret or hidden about the pool itself. Bartimaeus was nowhere to be seen, but then he suddenly appeared in the moonlight at the far end of the pool, standing outside a clump of Jericho balsams, a thick, leafy bush, whose branches tickled the water surface when the pool was full. The pool fluctuated in depth depending upon the season and whether the Gihon Spring was flowing. The spring waters were natural, but over the centuries, various pools and aqueducts had been constructed to manage the intermittent flow of the spring that sustained the life of the city.

I looked away from Bartimaeus and checked the streets for prying eyes, and when I looked back, the blind man had disappeared. Was he teasing? I headed toward the moonlit balsams, but stone abutments came near the edge of the pool in its midsection, necessitating entering the pool itself, which would explain why the balsams at the far end were rarely approached. I gingerly slipped into the water, which reached my armpits when I stood on the smooth-stone bottom. The pool grew deeper at the far end, and I swam the last few cubits.

When I arrived at the balsams, Bartimaeus was nowhere to be seen. I ploughed into the tangle of branches, but the deeper I went, the thicker the foliage. There was no obvious entrance to whatever it was that Bartimaeus was accessing, and then I came to solid rock. I was puzzled, and a moment of dread came over me. What if Bartimaeus was merely playing me for a fool, and there really was no underground exit? After a moment, I pushed aside the branches and returned to the small ledge where I had last seen Bartimaeus, and there the man stood with half a dozen other blind men from Jericho!

"Follow me," Bartimaeus said.

Bartimaeus slowly lowered himself into the pool, and I followed him down.

"Take hold of this rope and plug your nose with your other hand."

Bartimaeus dipped under the water and tugged me with him. At the lowest reaches of the pool, Bartimaeus slipped through a hewn tunnel, only a cubit in length, and we emerged on the far side of the rock wall into another pool, much smaller. I heard gurgling water where the spring fed the inner pool, which in turn filled the outer pool through the tunnel. Though I heard the water flow, I could see nothing. There was absolutely no light in this cavern, and only the instincts of a blind man could navigate the pitch darkness. Bartimaeus led me to an unseen rock ledge.

"We will wait here for the others."

Soon, I heard the splashes as heads bobbed up, and I could sense others near me even if I couldn't see them.

The watery entry explained why I had not been instructed to bring an oil lamp, but submersion would be a problem. I assumed that many would be frightened of the water. What of the children?

By touch and sound and smell and sheer instinct, Bartimaeus led the way into the inky blackness, followed by a snaking trail of men clutching a rope line. Bartimaeus led the way, and I followed. The other men brought up the rear. We navigated a winding labyrinth of passages. Sometimes our rocky path was dry, other times we waded through water. Sometimes we passed through narrow clefts in the rock walls and other times we were in huge caverns, indicated by the echo. My sense of sound became acute in the darkness. Sometimes I heard rats scurrying out of our way and other times I heard the rush of bat wings. In one place, we had to get on hands and knees to crawl through a tunnel several cubits in length. Sometimes we ascended, other times we descended. I lost all sense of time; we might have been traveling an hour or a day.

Bartimaeus and the others made no effort to remain silent. They laughed and argued when they came to a fork in the path, and Bartimaeus constantly uttered instructions.

When blackness gave way to a hazy gray, I assumed we neared the end of our journey. Signs of habitation increased, and finally we exited into the bright sunlight of the eastern sky. The cave entrance was within a rocky outcropping of a barren landscape, but Bartimaeus led me a short distance to a thin stretch of trees, a green slash on the mountainside.

"Welcome to my home," Bartimaeus said. "This is where the Jericho beggars live. The Jericho road runs along the ridge just above."

Bartimaeus explained that blind beggars had utilized this small, mountainside oasis adjacent to the Jericho road for generations. The beggars moved around their oasis with the ease of familiarity.

No one could remember how the cave connection to the Jerusalem underground had been first discovered; perhaps, this was indeed the secret entry point of David a millennium earlier, but Bartimaeus speculated that many things had changed over the centuries as rocks shifted and settled, and man-made pools and aqueducts altered the tributaries and courses of the massive spring system of the Jerusalem underground landscape.

"We'll spend the day here. Take and eat," Bartimaeus said, and he tore a loaf of bread in two and handed me the bigger piece. "We'll nap in the heat of the day and return to the city after the sun sets."

I wasted no time on sleep. I luxuriated in the sun and fresh air in the canyon. I gorged on fruit and gulped spring water. But, it was the road that led away from Jerusalem that held my fascination. Symeon was right; I could choose to head home to Damascus now and leave Jerusalem behind.

I climbed the steep, rocky path to the Jericho road above, and I hid in the boulders and watched as travelers trudged by. There weren't many in these troubled times. For thousands of years, wayfarers had passed this way, and the eternity of the place seeped into my bones. I crossed the road and climbed until I came to the high point along the mountain ridge. I perched atop a boulder and faced east. I refused to look west in the direction of Jerusalem. The Jordan River valley was beyond my view, but I sensed it as a rift in the undulating hills. The distant hills were on the far side of the Jordan. I imagined Moses sitting on a boulder in those far hills looking this way and longing for the land that had been promised. To the north and east, there was nothing to see except more undulating hills that shimmered in the haze, but I trusted that Damascus was there beyond the clouds, beckoning me away from the deathly stench of Jerusalem and toward home. Would I be safe, travelling alone? I have no money; how would I eat? Where would I sleep?

I hadn't expected the fresh air of freedom to be so intoxicating. My promise to return now seemed muddled--empty words I had spoken long ago in a strange place-- and the instincts of self-preservation welled within me. As the afternoon wore on, I blamed the others for their own fate. The bickering fools deserve what comes to them. They can choose to follow Bartimaeus to freedom if they wish; they don't need me to convince them. It's not my place anyway.

Already the sun was cooling on my back. It was time to move on. I stretched my legs and stood tall on the highest boulder in the land. Finally, I turned to face the setting sun that outlined the spires of Jerusalem, and I pissed in their direction before wheeling and heading east. I limped along at a slow pace and soon the falling darkness engulfed me.

As I moved down the road away from Jerusalem, pain forced me stop several times to rub my complaining knee, but each time I started again, it screamed the louder. Just as I was about to find a hiding spot to surrender to my knee's incessant protests, and perhaps succumb to sleep, the smells changed, the air cooled, and the roadway fell away beneath my feet as I approached the Jericho oasis. Rather than rest, I joined other creatures of the night in search of food and water. I found a pool of stagnant water soon enough; it was foul-smelling, but at least it was wet, and then I smelled bread, fresh bread baking on an open hearth, and I followed my nose. I peered from the shadows at a slope-shouldered hag in a hooded robe who shuffled about in the dark before dawn with only glowing charcoal to illuminate the stoop of her tumbledown hovel. Should I be beggar or thief?

I chose thievery. It was easier than facing the old woman, and when she disappeared into her hut, I leaped forward and scraped the small loaves into my outstretched tunic. I returned to the darkness and wolfed down the ill-gotten bread.

The piercing sun awakened me with a start. I had fallen asleep, leaning against a tree, and now my neck muscles were tied in knots, but my throbbing knee begged me to stay seated. I surveyed the trunk of the palm that had been my resting place only to discover that it was dead and barren.

I entered Jericho by walking along a Roman aqueduct that traversed a gully. Jericho was a fragrant and verdant city. Many springs bubbled up in the hills that sloped toward the Jordan River, still a few miles down the road to the east. Luxurious villas, country estates of the Jerusalem elite, peeked from the palms and ferns, but there was little activity, and traffic in

85

the marketplace was minimal as I followed the main road twisting along a creek headed toward the Jordan, which I reached by midday.

I hesitated to cross over, and it was not just the persistent pleading of knee pain; now, another ailment intruded on my escape. Perhaps from gorging on stolen bread, or maybe it was the stagnant water, but my stomach was unsettled. I left the trail and burrowed into a tangle of tumbleweeds that had snagged under a scraggly bush on the river's bank, and I sweated through the heat of the afternoon.

The Jordan was a boundary, real and symbolic. On the far side lay lands of the Gentiles and an uncertain fate. Was I ready to return to Damascus and face the memories that haunted me and the emptiness that would await me there? Somehow, I sensed that crossing over would have consequences beyond my knowing, for me, to be sure, but especially for the frightened faces of Anina's clan, huddling in Jerusalem and awaiting the good news that I promised to share. Despite the uncertainty, danger, and death that haunted the old Hebrew city, I sensed the presence of God-- not in the temple's holy of holies--but in that small band of Nazarenes. The deep serenity that filled my soul as Anina, the heir of Iesou, washed away my grime convinced me of that. Would the promises and hopes of their crucified leader die with them if they failed to survive the apocalypse that was sure to come to Jerusalem?

After the sunset and the arrival of the first star, I remembered the night sky on the eve of the battle of Beth Horon when I wondered which star was my own among the countless children of Abraham. Somehow, the stars were less comforting and more ominous on this night as I looked upward through the brambles, and when a shooting star fell from the sky, I sat upright, shuddered, and vomited my insides out. I was isolated and cut off, fallen from grace, more alone than I had ever felt.

I couldn't remember the last time I prayed, but I prayed then.

"You, Lord, reign forever; your throne endures to all generations. Why have you forgotten me completely? Why have you forsaken me these many days? Restore me to yourself, Lord, that I may be restored; show me your purpose, Lord, that I may follow; renew my days as of old--unless you have utterly rejected me, and are angry with me beyond measure, then do with me as you will."

I suppose I dosed for an hour or more, but a rustling in the bushes roused me; when I sat up, I heard only silence. I held my breath, and a branch snapped. I jumped up but couldn't see or hear anything, but I sensed an ominous presence: moving, circling, stalking. When I shifted, it stopped. When I hesitated, it moved. It was close, real close, but I couldn't see a thing in the blackness that filled the hollow like a drop of ink off the tip of my reed pen. Then came the roar of the wind, and the bushes shook, and branches crashed around me.

"Oof!"

A formless shape attacked me and knocked me to the ground, taking my breath away. Should I lie down with the worms and be still and be asleep and be dust? Why resist? What is the loss if I am only a speck tossed by the tempest into the current and carried away to the Dead Sea?

Yet, I continued the struggle whether survival instinct or choice. I shoved my right hand into the creature's face and barely held him off. We rolled in the dust, and he held me tight, but I wouldn't release him either. Although I could feel the beast's great strength, somehow, he did not overpower me, and we wrestled, and tangled, and spit, and cursed until the half-light of dawn, but neither of us gained an advantage over the other.

"Who are you?" His interrogation rumbled from deep in his gut and echoed across the river.

"I am no one," I said. "I am nobody."

"Do you have a name? What is your name?"

"I am Markos. My name is Markos."

"Ah, as I thought, you are Mars, the god of war."

My legs wrapped around his waist, and I squeezed tight.

"And who are you?" I gasped. "What is your name?"

"I am not the god of war," he replied.

His hands moved to my legs around his middle, and he wrenched my mangled knee as if he knew my weakness. I shrieked bloody spittle, but still I refused to release him.

"Sir give me your blessing," I demanded.

"You shall be Markos, the virile one, the father of many," he replied.

I unwrapped my legs and let him go. My lungs heaved as I raised myself on my elbows as he kissed my ruptured knee.

My eyes blinked as raindrops began to pelt down, and suddenly the apparition wasn't there. The sprinkles of rain soon grew into a torrent as the skies opened and poured water down upon me. At first, I sat and soaked and quenched my thirst. Then I arose, stripped down, and the rainwater washed over my nakedness. When the deluge ceased, the clouds disappeared, and a rainbow in the morning sun warmed the ground where I stood. All around me, the tumbleweeds came to life. Scraggly, dry stems and leaves unfolded and swelled into green ferns. My den became a bed of Jericho roses.

I didn't cross the Jordan that day; instead, I retraced my path back toward the oasis of the Jericho beggars and the secret entrance to Jerusalem. As I passed through a palm grove, something fell from a treetop and thumped on the ground next to me. I picked up a mottled green fruit with a dull white liquid seeping from a crack in the hard shell. I had never seen a coconut in these parts, but I suspected what it was. I smacked the husk against the tree trunk to widen the crack and let the sweet nectar drip slowly on to my tongue. When I swallowed, my throat was soothed, my belly stopped growling, and I walked without a limp.

Chapter Eleven

My face burst through the starlit veneer on the surface of the pool. I thanked Bartimaeus with a kiss on his forehead and swam past the stone abutments at the pool's center and climbed out. As I walked through the deathly shadows of the Jerusalem streets, my confidence in my decision remained solid. Soon, I was at Anina's door, then up the steps, and then I plopped down next to the familiar snores of Rufus and Alexander to get a few hours' sleep before the sunrise.

"Who's this? A ghost?"

Rufus and Alexander hovered over me with beaming faces.

I couldn't spill the good news fast enough. "It's true," I blurted out. "I made it safely all the way to Jericho."

Soon the rooftop verandah was abuzz. My journey with blind Bartimaeus improved my stature, even if my delayed return raised eyebrows, but no one asked. Did I glow? I felt so, and perhaps my own eagerness lessened the fears of the others. I was no longer merely the expendable water boy to be sent into the Jerusalem streets.

Anina kissed my cheek. "I knew you would find your purpose," she said.

Mishael, her husband, looked at me differently than before. For the moment, at least, hope overcame his suspicions of me.

"How many," he asked, "how many can safely travel at a time?"

Bartimaeus had suggested that each of five blind men could escort ten persons at a time.

"Half a hundred per night," I answered.

Mishael brought me to the men clustered around the oaken table, and I was peppered with questions.

"How soon can we begin?"

"Whenever we're ready."

"What can we bring with us?"

"Only what can be carried."

"What about the children?"

"They will be frightened, at first, but they can manage."

"What about the old and infirm?"

Before I could answer, one of the eldest in the group said he would remain behind with his invalid wife. "We were born here, and we shall die here, but knowing that my grandchildren will be safe is good news enough."

With each answer I sensed that hope swelled. There were doubters, to be sure, and some said they would stay and fight, but most of the Nazarenes would dare to escape. Symeon, the chosen leader of the twelve and Iesou's first cousin, remained silent until all the questions had been asked and answered, and then his booming voice proclaimed:

"Three days. You have three days to make your preparations. Sell what you can and sew your coins into your garments."

Then he turned to me and spoke to me directly for the first time.

"You shall lead the first group, along with your friends from Damascus. We shall cross the River Jordan to the land of the Gentiles, and you know their ways and their speech. You shall be our diplomat to make the way straight. The city of Pella is the nearest of the ten Greco-Roman cities on the far side of the Jordan, and that is where we shall gather. We will not assemble into a large group until we are safely across the river."

91

As Symeon finished speaking, a voice cried out. "Who shall be in the first exodus?"

After a brief silence, murmuring swelled to raucous disagreement until Anina climbed atop the oak table, and a hush fell over the verandah.

"Whoever wants to be first must be last of all and servant of all," she said, and she lifted a young baby in her arms. "Suckling mothers and infants shall be in the first group."

A few heads nodded, and the murmurs swelled again. Anina lifted her hands for silence.

"The rest shall be chosen by lot."

Mishael joined his wife on the table.

"Symeon and I will be in the last group," he said, and Symeon nodded his assent.

Mishael kissed his wife on her forehead. "You and your son shall be in the first group. You are the heirs of Yeshua," he said, and all the Nazarenes agreed.

Everyone would depart with only the clothes on their backs. The men folk sold all their possessions for the best price they could manage, and the wives frantically stitched gold and silver coins into tunics and robes. Foodstuffs fetched high prices, all else was virtually given away or left with those who stayed behind.

Three days later, there was an awkward moment when we departed and Mishael surrendered his family to my care. After he kissed his wife and son, he hesitated and then extended his hand toward me. "God be with you," he said.

In the fourth watch of the night, women, children, and a few young men, boys really, arrived at the pool by twos, threes, and fours. Groups of ten would depart that first night in five separate rope lines, each led by a blind man. As the first group assembled on the ledge near the Jericho balsams, I worried about the underwater entry, but I underestimated the courage of desperate persons, and I also underestimated the natural willingness of children for underwater dips. Nevertheless, heaping portions of encouragement would be doled out by trusting mothers and by Rufus, Alexander, and me when the mother's courage was thin. Bartimaeus brought Alexander into the passageway first to await the sputtering women and children who would emerge inside and assemble on the interior ledge.

Anina refused to follow Alexander into the water.

"I will await the last group tonight," she said. "I can see that I am needed on this ledge to encourage the mothers."

She was firm, and I didn't argue. I slipped into the water to join those waiting inside. Bartimaeus offered instructions, and the first group headed into the darkness, tightly clutching the rope that was their hope and their trust. I brought up the rear, leaving Rufus and Alexander for later groups.

We did not move silently. Bartimaeus shouted out directions. Some shrieked at the rats and the bats. And, there was a constant murmuring of mother to child: "don't be frightened," "mama is here," "we'll soon be there." Words of promise, encouragement, and exhortation filled the darkness, barely drowning out the whimpers of frightened children. The sounds from the groups behind echoed through the underground chambers.

In one cavern, Bartimaeus hesitated until all had entered.

"We are now beneath the temple," he announced. "The zealots are very close above us, but we are separated by tons of solid rock. Do you hear the running water? That is the temple water supply."

I took the time to piss in the zealots' drinking water.

The passage was inexorably slow. By the time the fuzzy shapes of the persons in front materialized, the children had grown silent. The initial tears of the innocents had given way to quiet trust. I carried a sleeping child in my arms for the last hour. As blue sky outside the cave entrance beckoned, the murmurs awakened the children who ran into the sunlight. Mothers sobbed. Some dropped to their knees and prayed.

When Bartimaeus delivered us to his oasis that was a green slash in the mountainside, the children discovered ripe figs, and laughter in the canyon replaced the whimpers of the caverns. Soon, the second group arrived, then the next and within an hour fifty Nazarenes had safely escaped from Jerusalem and arrived in the mountainside oasis along the Jericho road. True to her promise, Anina and Mattithyahu arrived with Alexander and the last group.

Safely out of Jerusalem, the journey to the land of the Gentiles would begin. After leaving a healthy stipend with Bartimaeus for services rendered by the blind men, we set out for Jericho, still a goodly distance down the rocky trail to the valley of the River Jordan. On the morrow, Bartimaeus and the beggars would escort another flight of escaping Nazarenes, and then again, and again, until all were safely out.

Initial chatter soon quieted. The harshness of the landscape mirrored our plight; though we had escaped the immediate dangers of civil war, these descendants of Jacob, "a wandering Aramaean," had undertaken an uncertain journey to return to the land of the Aramaeans. The mothers and their children were resolute but somber.

When we encountered others, we bunched together, and I kept my palm on the knob of the *gladius* that swung at my waist; for the first time, I was glad at the touch of the blade. All travelers on the Jericho road remained aloof. The bloodletting in Jerusalem roiled the entire countryside, and strangers nervously passed by other strangers, heads bowed low, eyes averted. Occasionally, packs of men on horseback galloped past, heading in either direction.

Our train of nearly three score persons moved slowly. Rufus and Alexander argued over our respective tasks, but I intervened; Rufus led the way, and I brought up the rear. Alexander moved back and forth offering encouragement. I frequently signaled the head to slow down; the slowest child set the pace for all. Anina and Mattithyahu fell in next to me, not because they were slow--the six-year-old boy was able to keep up--but because she wanted to continue our running conversation.

"Your friend who died to save you has also saved us," she said. "Are your doubts dispelled?"

I grunted without looking at her.

"And what of your sadness? Why do I suspect that your friend's death was merely the outer layer? Are you ready to peel away more?"

She was right, of course. My despair was deep and long-standing.

"I have witnessed many things--evil things--murder, brutality, and rape done in the name of the Lord," I said. "And I was not just a bystander. I belonged to the rebel mob that has brought Jerusalem to the eve of her doom."

95

"You are not the first soldier, and this was not the first army that failed to establish God's reign at the point of a sword."

We trudged along in silence for nearly a mile. At some point, she grasped my arm.

"I killed a defenseless man," I said. I was surprised to hear the words spill from my mouth, and I proceeded to tell her the story of the Roman aquilifer.

"I see," she said.

How could she see my dark heart? She is too pure and innocent to understand evil.

"War is sinfulness," she said, "and soldiers commit many sins; yet, they are victims, too." She squeezed my arm as her voice trailed off. "What war does to soldiers is a great evil."

With the sun setting at our backs, we began the gentle descent from the Jerusalem hills into the Jordan Valley. A cooling easterly breeze on our faces lifted the fragrances of the flowering oasis, and soon Jericho, the city of palms, came into view. After a hard, dusty journey that followed a sleepless night spent in the Jerusalem caverns, the Jericho oasis would be a welcome refuge.

When Rufus raised his hand signaling the end of our first day in a palm grove on the outskirts of the city, I plopped down at the edge of a bubbling, spring-fed rivulet. After I splashed cool, clear water on my face, I leaned against the trunk of a tall palm, lungs heaving, catching up with the emotion and exertion of the previous day and night; perhaps my breathing was merely keeping pace with the racing of my thoughts. Out of danger for the moment, the enormous difficulties facing these Nazarenes

96

would be overwhelming. The mood of the adults was sober, but children who had become cranky during the dry, dusty ordeal of the Jericho road, once again turned playful.

Rufus and I circulated and gathered a collection.

"There are plenty of ripe dates here. Fill your bellies," said Rufus.

Then we were off, striding purposefully toward the city's market, Rufus promising over his shoulder,

"We'll return soon with bread and whatever else we can scrounge up."

I had a short detour planned. We would visit the hut of the old woman whose bread I stole a week earlier and leave a few of our shekels with her. We found the hut straightaway, but the place was occupied by a young husband and wife and a pair of dusty-faced urchins who demonstrated their skill at misbehavior.

"No, no, there is not an old woman who lives here," the man said when I asked for the hag whose bread I had stolen.

I surveyed the scene again; perhaps this was the wrong hovel. No, the hearth was there, the stoop was there, everything was as I remembered, except for the hooded woman who made bread in the darkness before dawn. Rufus gave me a look that said he doubted my recollection, and I too was mystified as we continued toward the market. I placed a single shekel into the palm of each child anyway.

Hours after Rufus and I returned with stale bread and sour-smelling garum, a fermented fish sauce, snores filled the cool night air, and I slept well under a bright sky.

"Get up." The voice of Rufus seemed to come from a far-off place. "Wake up, the sun will soon rise."

I rolled over in my rumpled robe. It still seemed dark night with glimmers of dawn silhouetting sleeping hills across the Jordan River and the tall outlines of Rufus and Alexander standing side-by-side with their backs to me, emptying their night bladders and arguing, of course. As I leaned forward to tie my sandals onto my feet, I winced at the raw blisters. It would be a long day.

The travelers gulped down the remaining loaves and garum and drank deeply of the spring water. We would replenish our food daily with purchases from the villages we passed through. I assumed my customary position at the rear of the pack as we set out down the road to the east. Soon, we would cross over the River Jordan, and we would travel the east bank as the trail followed the river to the north. With children, our pack moved slowly. Before long, the sun's first rays warmed our faces and awakened high spirits, and when we reached the Jordan River, the entire entourage splashed in the shallows.

The days melted together, but by the fourth day, even the energy and enthusiasm of the children had dissipated. From my position at the rear, I became the encourager to keep spirits up and stragglers moving, but my brave face and exhortations belied my own fears. My feet blistered, and my belly growled for want of food. Slight of build and of stamina, I envied the fit bodies of the brothers from Damascus. Even in our childhood, I struggled, and they thrived in the athletic contests.

On the last day's journey, a young man joined me in the rear. He listened but never spoke during the discussions of the twelve under the verandah, but under the noonday sun, talk spilled out. With only one set of ears to hear him speak, he jabbered.

"We will fight; we are not cowards," he said. "When the mashiah returns, the prophet Isaiah promises that 'destruction is decreed. 'The Lord God of hosts will make a full end in all the earth.'"

Although I had never read the scrolls of old, I knew well the Hebrew expectation of a warrior-king to be sent by God to destroy the enemies of the Hebrew people and establish God's reign on earth. This was standard fare for the Jewish worldview. For the Nazarenes and for the Pauline network of Gentile congregations spread across the regions of the Great Sea, including the congregation in Damascus, this was also common understanding but with the further claim that Yeshua was the one: the anointed, the mashiah, the christos. He was proclaimed to be the shoot from the stump of Jesse, the branch that grew out of his roots, the son of David, as blind Bartimaeus had said.

I said nothing, and my silence seemed to encourage the young man's rant.

"When the trumpet sounds, we will take up arms and join God's holy battle."

"What if Jerusalem is doomed?" I asked without making eye contact. "What if the Romans win?"

"Well, just wait," the young man stammered.

Power to the powerless. Order amidst chaos. Such hopes seemed distant, and the reign of God seemed far off. I paused and gazed at the River Jordan. My companion stopped a few paces ahead. I picked up a pebble and tossed it into the center of the stream. The current carried the ripples away.

"I don't believe Yeshua was the mashiah," I mumbled under my breath. "At least not in the way you think."

99

"What? What did you say?"

I shook my head signifying that I had said nothing important, and I again trudged ahead. I was glad that my words had been carried away by the river and that the young Nazarene hadn't heard me. He would have been shocked. I shocked myself.

Pella 68 CE

Then Moses went up from the plains of Moab to Mount Nebo, to the top of Pisgah, which is opposite Jericho, and the LORD showed him the whole land: "This is the land of which I swore to Abraham, to Isaac, and to Jacob, saying, 'I will give it to your descendants'; I have let you see it with your eyes, but you shall not cross over there." Then Moses, the servant of the LORD, died there in the land of Moab, at the LORD's command.

Joshua [Yeshua] son of Nun was full of the spirit of wisdom, because Moses had laid his hands on him; and the Israelites obeyed him, doing as the LORD had commanded Moses. After the death of Moses, the servant of the LORD, the LORD spoke to Joshua son of Nun, Moses' assistant, saying, "My servant Moses is dead. Now proceed to cross the Jordan, you and all this people, into the land that I am giving to them, to the Israelites."

Selections from Deuteronomy chapter 34 and Joshua chapter 1

Chapter Twelve

We arrived, or nearly so. Our weary band of travelers encamped on the banks of the Jordan along the roadway that headed into the hills and the valley of Pella, our hoped-for home, at least until Jerusalem was again safe. Perhaps, it would be longer than that. We had departed Judea, skirted Samaria, and the southeast tip of the Galilee was just across the river. The evening sun cast a warm, orange glow on the eastern hills. Haze from the smoke of many hearths hung in a sheet over a green valley.

Pella was a city of the Decapolis, a loose grouping of Greco-Roman cities to the east of Palestine, adjacent to the Nabatean kingdom. The Nabateans were Arabs, and their kingdom scraped against the shifting, eastern frontier of the Roman Empire. Local lore said Alexander the Great passed this way with his army of conquest, renaming the oasis community "Pella" after his own birthplace in Macedonia. Since that time nearly four centuries earlier, the area retained a strong Hellenic influence with a mixed populace of Arabs, Jews, Aramaeans, Persians, and more than a few Greeks and Romans. Located in a lush oasis near caravan routes of commerce, the city enjoyed a steady prosperity.

"Thank you, sir."

I turned to face the soft voice.

"Thank you for helping us find our way."

Young Mattithyahu spoke while clutching the security of his mother's robe.

"Go ahead, son, give him your gift."

The youngster looked into his mother's eyes, pleading for courage. Anina took him by the hand, and they both stepped forward to present me with a plum. Its softness and rich purple hue said it was ripe. I bit into it and laughed as yellow juice dribbled into my beard. When I finished, I rinsed my face in the river and returned for conversation with droplets of water clinging to my reddish beard.

"I, too, wish to thank you," Anina said. "When Mishael, my husband, catches up to us in a few days, I'm sure he will thank you also."

I wasn't so sure. Mishael had barely concealed his suspicion of the Hellenists from Damascus. True enough, he had trusted me to gather food in dangerous Jerusalem, to scout escape routes, and to lead the flock of Nazarenes through the underground tunnels of Jerusalem, but what would happen when I ceased to be useful?

"Each of us must decide whether creation is good or evil and then act accordingly," she said as she gathered my hands into her own. "You have led us to safety. I think you have decided."

It seemed so.

We sat down in the shade of a sprawling willow tree.

"My mother is a Gentile," I said. "What is more, my parents didn't have me circumcised as an infant. I'm still not circumcised."

"I assumed that," she said. "Do you think that matters to me? Or, to God?"

She giggled. Her round face encircled by curly locks that sneaked out from her scarf seemed a natural landscape for grins and giggles.

"Well, perhaps it matters some to my husband, but we've already crossed the river, haven't we?"

"And my name is not Menachem. It is Markos."

She didn't seem surprised or offended. "I don't know that name," she said. "What is its meaning?"

I did not share either meaning; one derived from Mars, God of war, and the other--"the virile one, the father of many" --had been assigned weeks earlier when I wrestled on the far shore of the river. Both were embarrassing.

"I don't think it has a meaning," I said. "It's just a name."

"I shall call you Markos, but I shall still think of you as the Comforter."

Mattithyahu moved to the bank of the Jordan and tossed pebbles into the flowing stream.

"That one will be my only child," Anina said. "There were several stillborn before Mattithyahu, and the midwife who delivered him said there would be no more. It is no longer the way of women for me. Mishael is such a good father, and he deserves many sons, which I cannot give him."

A tear streaked her dusty cheek and curled around a wan smile.

"Life is unfair," I said.

I didn't intend to be brusque, merely honest, but I immediately regretted my flippant comment. Her brown eyes flashed wide then quickly narrowed and bore into my own. I looked away.

"I think I misjudged you," she said. "Yes, you are sad, but more than that, I believe you are angry. What irks you so?"

Damn her persistent questioning. I joined her son throwing stones into the river, and I aimed at an eddy swirling around an unseen obstruction beneath the water's surface. After a few moments of silence, I spoke with my back to her.

"Damascus is a grand old city, a lush oasis in the foothills of snow-capped mountains where the sweet scent of jasmine flavored my life, and I had a life, a good life. As a boy, my parents allowed me to study at grammar school, and later the city's favorite scribe mentored me and introduced me to many of the city's leading citizens; one of them saw promise in me and arranged a marriage with his oldest daughter."

Anina was right; I felt the anger surging within me. I flung a rock all the way to the far side of the river, and I wheeled to face her.

"My wife died giving birth to our first child," I blurted the words almost as an accusation. "Why did my blessing turn into a curse? Why did fullness become empty? Why did the whirlwind whisk away the breath from my sweet, gentle, and innocent young bride, the very essence of purity?"

By now, my words were choking me, and I cleared my throat.

"My son's first--and last-- gulp of air was sucked into the dust."

I turned back to the river and squatted on my haunches. My words became a whisper.

"I was a husband and nearly a father. Life held hope and promise, but who am I now?"

Anina kneeled at my side and reached her hand to brush away a wayward lock of hair from my forehead. After a moment's silence, she spoke.

"I pray for the day when you can forgive God ... and yourself."

Chapter Thirteen

The next morning, I became a diplomat. Now that the Nazarene women and children had arrived on the banks of the Jordan in the outskirts of Pella, my first task would be to speak to the magistrates on behalf of the refugees from Jerusalem. As a scribe in Damascus, I understood Roman law and Hellenistic customs, and that was precisely why the Nazarenes chose me and my friends from Damascus to lead the way.

"Look at my tattered robes," I said. "The magistrates will think me a beggar, not an emissary."

It was true enough, but Rufus and Alexander looked no better. We decided to leave Rufus in charge of our camp while Alexander and I trekked the short distance into Pella. As the sun rose high over the eastern hills, we followed the well-worn road leading to the city of Pella, a free city of the Roman Empire, whose citizens chose their own leaders.

Flourishing vineyards and wooden granaries nestled in the folds in the hills testified to the fertile land, favorable climate, and plentiful water. Outlying villages and settlements supported the city proper, and soon the road into Pella broadened into the *Decumanus Maximus*, the principal east-west oriented street of a planned Roman city. We passed by warehouses, public baths, and a fountain house where a spring bubbled up to nourish the citizenry.

To be sure, Pella predated the arrival of the Romans; indeed, humans had inhabited this valley for thousands of years. There were rumors of a major Canaanite temple here before the time of King David. Later, the Greeks built a city--guarded by a fortress at the highest point in the hills--before Roman armies destroyed it over a century before we arrived, and now it was the Romans' turn to enjoy the benefits of these environs, but it

106

wasn't only Romans or Greeks; a diverse populace coexisted and contributed to mutual prosperity. There was plenty for all--at least, that is what we hoped.

As we approached the intersection with the *Cardo Maximus*, the main street along a north-south axis, the wooden buildings gave way to stone arches and columns, with a covered stoa enclosing a commercial square that the Romans called the *forum* and the Greeks called the *agora*.

"Sausages!" "Barley beer!" "Goatskins!"

Cries of hawkers, braying donkeys, and crowing roosters greeted our arrival at city center. A strange admixture of aromas--goat dung, wood smoke, perfume from the orient, and more--teased our noses. The stalls of the stoa included merchants selling wine, herbs and spices, vegetables, and separate vendors for fish, cattle, pork, and mutton. Farmers from the countryside offered livestock on the hoof. Shops for artisans and craftsmen mixed in.

We stopped at the portable brazier of a pudding vendor: a heavyset woman who seemed to wear her entire wardrobe in layers. One heavy-lidded eye was sightless, and the old woman stared cockeyed at us with her good eye. Sausages and onions sizzled over her charcoal. We bought sausages, but we really sought information.

"Tell us, good woman, where might we find the city magistrate?" I asked in my finest Greek.

The woman's jaw ruminated on her answer like a cow chewing its cud. Her single eye surveyed the dirty and tattered clothing of the strangers who stood before her.

"Don't know if'n our magistrates have the time for the likes of you," she replied in Aramaic, the spoken language of many of the Semitic

107

peoples of the region, including the Jews and the Nabateans, but with a dialect that jarred my ears.

She leaned over and plucked uncooked sausages from a vase and plopped them onto the brazier to replace the ones we chomped down. When she straightened up, she placed her right hand on the backside of her hip as if she pushed her bones back into place and pointed with a crooked finger on her left hand.

"That's Cyrus right over there. He holds court with the citizens every afternoon for an hour or two. If'n he feels like it, he might talk to you. He's the chief magistrate."

The uncovered blonde hair and clean-shaven face of Cyrus said his homeland was far to the west. He seemed to have a hard time listening to the complaints of one of his citizens; perhaps that was always true, or perhaps he was distracted by the pair of unkempt strangers who waited their turn to speak.

"We're refugees from Jerusalem," I explained when Cyrus greeted us. "We're here because we chose not to fight the Roman armies."

"Out of loyalty or fear?" Cyrus asked with a wry smile.

I lied. I wasn't about to mention my role as a warrior against the Roman legion at Beth-Horon. "Though none of us have ever been disloyal to the emperor, I confess that our motives are less about allegiance to the crown than to protect our wives and children. We respect the authority and power of Rome, but we are nonpartisan."

I was interrupted by the citizen who had been complaining to Cyrus

"Refugees? Hah, you're spies and assassins!"

His eyes bulged wide and black, and spittle spewed from his mouth as he ranted.

"Thieves! You'll steal from us!"

Obviously, the man had not seen our rag-tag band of women and children, but I doubted that he was interested in the truth of our plight. Cyrus the magistrate intervened. Placing a strong hand on the man's shoulder, he turned him away from us and led him a few paces down the street where they continued in animated and profane discussion.

"They come to rape our women!"

Finally, the man stomped off, shaking his fist at us as he departed. "They'll murder us in our sleep!"

Cyrus returned to us and spoke as his gaze followed the man.

"You must forgive him. Like many in our city, he is frightened by the events across the river. We're not bad people, but fear breeds hateful behavior towards refugees." The magistrate grunted. "Truth be told," he said, "our free city also fears Roman imperial overreaching."

Cyrus' eyes probed my own.

"How many are you?"

"We are only fifty women and children now, but more will be joining us. Perhaps several hundred if all arrive safely."

Cyrus pursed his lips and sucked in a breath with a slight whistle.

"Are your people law-abiding?"

"There are no thieves among us."

"Are you hardworking and industrious?"

"We count artisans and craftsmen among our number. I myself am a trained scribe. We will be self-sufficient additions to your city. Right now, we're anxious to buy food and wares from your merchants."

I extended my arm and made a sweeping gesture toward the marketplace. My positive tone belied my uncertainty about how long the collective funds of the Nazarene refugees would last.

Cyrus cleared his throat as he paced around us, looking first in one direction, then another. Finally, he pointed and said,

"The *Odeon* is that way. It is a theater in a hillside. Your people may encamp on the far side of that hill--out of sight of the theater, mind you-- but if there are troublemakers among you, your entire community will bear the consequences of misbehavior."

With a slight nod, he started to leave but offered a final word of caution.

"Be vigilant for your safety," he said, and then he left us standing alone. I instinctively felt for my sword at my side, but we had left our weapons in our camp.

Our settlement on the edge of the city swelled daily as each group of Nazarene refugees arrived; when the last wave led by Symeon and Mishael pushed into camp late one evening, they pulled a cart behind. They had encountered a farmer on the road and purchased his supply of barley beer, the first fruits of the spring harvest.

I was there when the last group, including the Nazarene leaders, arrived. I waited while Mishael picked up his son under his armpits and tossed him in the air, and then I waited while Mishael and Anina embraced. Her quaking shoulders said she sobbed in her husband's arms. After she wiped her cheeks with the folds of her robe, she took her husband by his hand and delivered him to me. Mishael reached out with both hands and clasped the right hand I extended. He pulled me to the cart and poured two cups of beer. He handed one to me and raised his own cup and offered a slight nod of the head. We drained our cups, slapped each other on the back, and went our separate ways. No words were spoken.

The happy hoots of survival sounded on the hillside until the dawn peaked over the hills, and the last revelers passed out on the grass.

Soon, the settlement had the makings of a small village. A few tents appeared, and several men pooled their resources to purchase half a dozen dams and a sire to begin a goat herd. Other men purchased a bred cow. Getting settled proved difficult. Unskilled men hired out as day laborers for minimal wages and only found work a day or two per week. Even skilled artisans found meager employment. Older women took in laundry or sewing, and younger women worked as servants for wealthy merchants of the city, but the pay was scant and sporadic--often mere table scraps. A few of us set up our own shops in the forum and hoped for clientele.

With a small stall near the fountain house, I became a scribe once again, a merchant of ink strokes on a papyrus roll. I would write contracts of marriage and of commerce for a fee. My marks recorded inventories, transactions, and important events.

In the early days, Symeon set watches who kept bonfires burning through the night, but as spring turned into summer without incident, it seemed we were safe, and the practice died out. True to the magistrate's warning, we often encountered hostility, but we endured the icy looks and veiled jibes from the locals as the price that refugees must pay.

Soon after the arrival of the last contingent of escaped Nazarenes, another diplomatic mission was arranged. This time, I merely accompanied Mishael and Symeon who introduced their people to the local synagogue leader. Large numbers of Jews had resided in Pella for generations, and they were solidly entrenched in the community.

How could we sing the Lord's song in a foreign land? The psalmist had asked this question when the Jews of Jerusalem were exiled to Babylon five centuries earlier. The synagogue was the answer: instead of temple--Torah; instead of priests--rabbis; instead of sacrifice--study.

The synagogue was near the city center, and its outward appearance was no different than other public buildings, except for one construction feature. All the other buildings faced the east-west or north-south configuration of the streets, but the synagogue was canted. The impressive front of the building--with columns, a portico, and double doors--faced toward Jerusalem, which lay to the southwest.

We bounded up the steps, between Doric columns, and paused while I read a Greek inscription posted near the doorway.

Theodotus, son of Vettenos the priest and an archisynagogos [synagogue leader], son of an archisynagogos, and grandson of an archisynagogos, who built the synagogue for the reading of Torah and for studying the commandments, and the hostel, chambers, and the water installations for lodging needy strangers, and whose father, with the elders and Simonidus, founded the synagogue.

We stepped inside. Three rows of benches lined each side of the perpendicular room, each row sitting atop the one below in ascending fashion. The synagogue was empty except for an old man who was preoccupied reading a scroll placed upon a wooden platform, the Torah shrine, in the center of the hall. He wore a skull cap, as I did, with long and scraggly gray hair dangling behind and a matching beard. As we

112

approached, his face was up close against the scroll, and he whispered the words as he read.

"What!" His head jerked up, and then he laughed at himself. "I didn't hear you coming. I'm afraid you gave me a start," and he laughed again. He climbed down from a tall, three-legged stool, and approached his visitors. He was short and stooped.

"We are refugees from Jerusalem," Symeon said, "and we have settled on the outskirts of the city, near the theater."

"Yes, yes. So, I heard. My name is Rafael. And you are ...?" As each of his visitors introduced himself, Rafael mouthed their names, and a quick nod registered them in his memory.

"I'm what passes for a rabbi, I suppose, but I'm a poor one," Rafael said. "Most of my life I was a wine merchant, and I have no formal training in the holy books, but I have been appointed to be the leader of the Jews of this synagogue for no better reason than I'm old and willing to do it. When old Theodotus passed on, he left no one to replace him, except a poor wine merchant nephew." He chuckled again.

In the days that followed, I would get to know the old wine merchant well when he would stop to chat on his daily visit to the fountain house to fill a jar with water.

"Have you come for my blessing? Well, you shall have it," Rafael said as he turned and headed toward an anteroom. "Now that we have our business out of the way, perhaps you'd eat a bite with me? It's early in the day for wine, but I can offer you fresh baked loaves dipped in dill-spiced yogurt."

As we munched on his treats, his visage darkened.

"I must be honest," he said. "I will be your friend and ally, but not every Jew of Pella will be so welcoming. Some will ask why you fled rather than fight for mother Jerusalem. Some will see you as competitors within our local economy. It will be good if you come and pray with us on the Sabbath to assure those who wonder about your sect."

Cyrus the magistrate welcomed us but warned that his citizenry feared our presence and cautioned us to be vigilant for our safety. Now, Rabbi Rafael hinted that even the Jews would harbor suspicions of the Nazarene refugees.

We were strangers in a strange land.

Chapter Fourteen

On a bright, cool morning, I bade farewell to my friends from Damascus. We climbed to the highest point around Pella in the range overlooking the Jordan River Valley to visit the ruins of the Greek fortress there, but I really wanted to send them off in private. Except for the shepherds who minded their flocks of sheep and goats, we were alone.

"Go to your wives and children, as you should," I said, "but I shall remain in Pella. At least, for now."

No one spoke as we sat in the ruins on stones hauled to this hilltop by persons long dead. A few wispy clouds sailed on a sea-blue sky. From our vantage, we could see the whole Sea of Galilee less than a day's journey to the northwest, and mountains shimmered in the haze far to the west on the coast of the Great Sea. In between lay the hills and plains of the Galilee, and the home of Iesou of Nazareth and of the false mashiah, Eleazar ben Simon. Somewhere to the southwest, far beyond our view, Jerusalem perched high in the Judean hill country. From afar, the lands seemed entirely peaceful, belying the violence up close.

"Is that Mt. Hermon?" Rufus asked with disbelief.

"Of course not," Alexander replied, not willing to acknowledge his brother's discovery.

But, indeed, it was the familiar mountain range of our youth. All eyes turned to the north. The three peaks of snow-capped Mt. Hermon were the greatest mountains of the entire region. From this distance, about seventy miles, the mountain seemed benign enough, but up close the peaks towered over our Damascus homeland like white-haired eminences presiding over their domain. Many peoples and their gods had celebrated or feared Mt. Hermon, a "mountain set apart" according to the Hebrews.

The headwaters to the Sea of Galilee and the River Jordan were to be found in the foothills flowing southwest, and the Barada River flowed east out of the mountains and spilled into the Ghouta Oasis of Damascus.

"Why would you remain in Pella?" asked Alexander. "Return with us to Damascus, our home and yours. Your mother's hearth beckons."

The sight of the familiar mountain tugged at me. I offered a hollow response.

"I am single, and I have no family. You have responsibilities there; perhaps I'll join you soon," I said, but I wasn't sure, nor was I sure of my own mind.

Rufus took my side. "He has his reasons. Who are we to question?"

Much too soon, it was time for my friends to depart.

"Please deliver this letter to my mother," I said as my voice cracked, "and read my words to her."

Charis was like other mothers and could not read, but then very few men had learned that skill either. Rufus, Alexander, and I were among the very few, less than one in ten, who had been allowed the privilege of literacy; while our peers were required to work at an early age, we attended Greek grammar school until our early teens. I handed my compatriots a small papyrus scroll for my mother in which I told her I was well and promised to return one day soon. My hand softly brushed against theirs, and then they were gone.

I didn't immediately return to the city. The solitude of the ruins encircled by a vast horizon invited contemplation. The hours slipped away as I wandered among the stones.

Thoughts of Damascus were sweeter than they had been since … well, since before the whirlwind. Certainly, the hole in my heart over the death of my wife and child hadn't healed, and the cries of bawling lambs in my mother's court still haunted me, but I also remembered the taste of my mother's loaves dipped in honey and washed down with warm goat's milk. I reached behind my ear and my reed pen was there where it belonged. I had already scribed a few contracts from my cramped stall in Pella, and I was pleased that I had done good work.

And what of this Nazarene band of refugees? Serendipity brought us together. Rehum sacrificed his life for my own, a brave stable master provided a hideout, Anina and the others offered sanctuary, and then a blind beggar led all of us to safety. Without such good fortune, would these friends, family, and followers of the man from Nazareth survive? Or, was it more than mere chance?

I had known of the Nazarenes from my childhood. Their scrupulosity had been mocked in my Hellenist synagogue in Damascus.

"You must not eat this or that," the Nazarenes proclaimed. "You must observe the Sabbath, and your male babies must be circumcised precisely on the eighth day after their birth."

What did it all boil down to? "Do not do as the Gentiles do," which to the Hellenist congregation of Iesou followers in Damascus sounded like, "you're not good enough."

Yet, they took me in, and now I was curious. I had heard stories of Iesou from the Nazarenes--"Yeshua" they called him--that were unknown in my Damascus community. With our escape and resettlement now accomplished, perhaps I would have the opportunity to dig deeper.

As a youngster, I never pondered my congregation in Damascus; our rituals, our liturgy, and our sacred stories were unquestioned presuppositions for one born into the community of the followers of Iesou

117

in Damascus. The whirlwind had changed all that. Along with my innocence, trust and faith had been whisked away in the dust storm, and doubt and despair had rushed in. And now? Now I wasn't sure, but I wondered.

More than anything, Anina kept me here in Pella. She inspired her people. She was calm. She was hope. She was trusted. When a young boy burned himself in a bonfire, her poultice healed his arm without scabbing. When a servant girl returned without pay, Anina stormed the master's courtyard, and she scolded the day's wage and more out of the miser. A well-known face in the market, she would drive a shrewd bargain but then leave an extra copper coin with the vendor. In the evenings, she spread a large blanket covered with bread, cabbages, carrots or other seasonal vegetables, and the hungry among us supped with her. Under her dogged questioning, the rotting pus that oozed deep in my heart had spilled out. She said there was good in me. She said I had a purpose.

As dusk descended on the stones, I headed down the path toward Pella following a bright star in the western sky. According to Hebrew tradition, the evening star was the son of dawn. I thought differently; the star was a woman, the daughter of the heavens.

Chapter Fifteen

The tale-teller stuttered. Everyone around the Pella forum knew the shriveled old man. Hunched over a hollow belly, the man dressed like a slave with loincloth and headdress but no sandals, robes, or tunic. The worn goatskin bag slung over his bony shoulder undoubtedly carried the sum of the man's possessions. He was not a resident of Pella, nor had he been among the Nazarenes who escaped through the tunnels under Jerusalem, but he wandered into the city alone, apparently a refugee from the Galilee. If the man had a name, it was unknown, and even the trouble-making urchins of the marketplace called him "tale-teller".

"He-hello ch-ch-children."

"He-hello t-t-tale t-teller," replied the ringleader, and the brats would hoot and scamper, each of them mimicking his stutter.

He didn't seem to mind. He would simply readjust his bag on his back, and hobble off on his wiry bow-legs, with a smug smile that hinted there was more to the man than first appearances.

I also carried a goatskin sack slung over my back that contained my inks and papyrus scrolls. I no longer slept under the stars in the Nazarene settlement but on a goatskin mat in a lean-to, barely a closet, attached to the backside of a mud-brick dwelling near the fountain house and the stall where I plied my trade as a scribe. My landlady was a Jewess, and she sometimes left yesterday's bread on my mat.

I first spoke with the stuttering man on my way to the fountain house to fill my water skins.

"Tell me, why are you called the tale-teller?"

The man said nothing but turned to face me. His headdress was partially unwrapped, and the end seemed alive as it snapped in the breeze.

A melon-slice smile spread across a burnished face, revealing a single tooth jutting up from the lower jaw. The man ritually rubbed his tongue across the tooth, preparing to speak. He slowly lifted his face to the sun, closed his eyes, extended his arms outward and upward, and drew a deep breath.

"The reign of God is like a mustard seed, which, when sown upon the ground, is the smallest of all the seeds on earth."

The tale-teller spoke clearly without a hint of impediment.

"Yet when it is sown it grows up and becomes the greatest of all shrubs," the voice was full and rich, with a sing-song tone to the telling, "and puts forth large branches, so that the birds of the air can make nests in its shade."

I was as confused as the small crowd that listened to the sweet sounds of the tale-teller, the one who stuttered in normal speech.

"Th-this is a p-p-parable of Yeshua," he said, "I t-told it in the s-synagogue in Capernaum." The smile on his face stretched to his ear lobes.

And that was how I became friends with the tale-teller, one in a long tradition of oral storytellers whose memorized recitations passed the important stories from one generation to the next. I scribed what the tale-teller uttered. The scribbles became mine, not an inventory for a merchant or a wedding contract for a father, but my own marks, a little trail of myself in ink strokes on sheets of papyrus.

I also encouraged the Nazarenes to repeat their well-worn stories. The old generation--those who had walked with Yeshua in Galilee, those who had broken bread with the man, those who mourned his brutal death on the cross, and those who were caught up in the wildfire of pentecost with reports of a resurrected mashiah--had mostly passed on, but their sons and daughters, and their grandsons and granddaughters, were counted among those who now encamped in the outskirts of Pella. And there were always new arrivals, refugees from this place or that, who found their way to Pella, often with their family or friends. I listened with a keen ear to the stories that I recorded with my reed pen and papyrus.

What I heard often surprised me.

I was born of believers and baptized as a baby, but I knew only the passion story in which Iesou was crucified but rose from the dead--for such was the liturgy of my Damascus congregation. The second and third-hand accounts I now heard provided a biography of a different sort, the story of a flesh and blood human who hiked the back roads of the Galilee, a preacher, a teacher, perhaps a prophet, perhaps a revolutionary.

Who was this man?

The most curious refrain I heard was the voice of regret.

"If only Yeshua had lived."

"If only Yeshua was here today."

"If only the damned Romans hadn't murdered him."

I had been raised in a community that celebrated the death of Iesou, who believed he died a horrible death on the cross as a ransom for many, that ritually drank his blood poured out for many, but why did these Jews from Palestine lament his death? Was there no meaning to his suffering? And his death? Why didn't they understand? Did they not have eyes to see and ears to hear? Yeshua walked with them, he taught them, and they heard him speak to the masses.

Who did they say he was?

"T-t-there's another s-scribe in P-P-Pella," the tale-teller said to me one day when we met at the fountain house.

I asked around and soon found the man named Quintus. The man was not unfriendly, and he willingly shared his story.

Quintus was a Greek-speaking Jew from Caesarea by the sea, the Greco-Roman enclave in Palestine that was the home to governors and kings who resided in the palace built by Herod the Great and a two-day journey from the coast to Jerusalem. Quintus' roots were in the Caesarea community of Hellenists, Jews who spoke Greek rather than Aramaic and whose dress, diet, and manner of life seemed more Gentile than Hebrew. Many of these were followers of Iesou, whose forbearers had escaped from Jerusalem following the stoning of Stephen the Hellenistic martyr. Quintus himself had recently fled Caesarea when the Roman General Vespasian swept the city clean of Jews after making the city his headquarters while his armies prepared to march on Jerusalem.

Quintus wasn't a scribe but a merchant who led camel caravans from the seaport, across the coastal plain, and into the hill country of Judea with wares bound for the inland city of Jerusalem. By chance, he once heard someone repeat the words of Iesou, and Quintus jotted the saying down in the margin of his ledger of accounts. On his next trip to Jerusalem, it happened again, and soon his ledgers were filled with sayings alongside his business ciphers. The sayings were on the lips of many, but Quintus was alone in recording them with pen and ink. Some of his sources claimed to have heard the words directly from the mouth of Iesou, but most of the sayings recorded by Quintus had been oft-repeated by the time Quintus scribed them in his ledgers.

"I've accumulated quite a few over the years," Quintus said.

122

"May I see them? May I copy them?" I asked.

"No, they're not ready for public view yet. They're just my scribbles alongside my journal entries, but I plan to rewrite them with great care. Then you and others may look."

"When will that be?"

"Soon, but I will wait until I reach Antioch, which is where I'm heading."

Antioch of Syria was the greatest city of the eastern end of the Great Sea--save Alexandria in Egypt--and boasted the largest colony of Iesou followers outside of Jerusalem. Following three years in Damascus, Paulos the apostle had spent a dozen years in Antioch. I had no intention of traveling to Antioch, even though Quintus' scribbles intrigued me. When I depart Pella, it will be for Damascus, not Antioch.

Chapter Sixteen

Then came the day when a wealthy refugee arrived in Pella. The entourage of Yosef ben Yosef included Hannah his wife, Hava his sole child and her husband, Abner, several nieces and nephews, and more than a dozen servants. Each family member sat astride a camel, and several female servants managed a string of donkeys laden with possessions stripped from their villa in Arimathea, a small Judean city in the hill country a day's journey north of Jerusalem. Yosef had fared better in Arimathea than the aristocrats in Jerusalem who lost wealth--or their lives--at the hands of the zealots, but now he fled Judea before the conflagration would engulf his own city and estate. Each of the male servants stood tall upon a muscular frame with a lance hoisted onto a shoulder and a short sword sheathed at the waist. Yosef's clan encamped in colorful tents along the road to the River Jordan, and his generosity improved the lot of many in the Nazarene settlement, but rumors of trouble within the household soon proved true.

I was lost in my thoughts, and the shadow that fell across my scroll startled me. I squinted up at a faceless man in a tall hat framed by the sun. I stood up and stepped to the side to see who had come to my stall. The man I faced was quite short, but his turban made him a full head taller. The turban was stitched with fine cloth and banded in gold leaf that matched the long robes worn by the diminutive man. The headpiece alone was worth more than a scribe would earn in a year. A single bodyguard accompanied the rich man, standing with arms crossed, watching and waiting from an appropriate distance.

"He's a damn fool, and he'll lose his head. And for what? I'll spit on his grave," the visitor said. He spat on the dusty street for emphasis.

I listened but did not respond; I assumed the man would get around to his point soon enough.

"And me, an old man with only a daughter but no heirs. This young generation has no respect, no honor, and no responsibility."

Finally, the rich visitor shut one eye and squinted at me with the other. Thick, bushy eyebrows accented his eye movements.

"You are the scribe?"

I nodded.

"A good one?"

I shrugged. "As good as any, I suppose."

For a few seconds, the man rolled his lower lip in a pout and stroked the gray beard on his chin. "Well, I guess you'll do. I hear you're a follower of Yeshua, so you'll be sympathetic to my dilemma."

I pulled out a fresh papyrus scroll, moistened the tip of my reed, and rubbed the wet tip across a cake of dry soot that served as my black ink. When I was ready, I searched the man's face, awaiting his instructions.

"I am Yosef ben Yosef", the man said, but I already assumed as much.

"I need a bill of divorce … for my daughter. Hava is her name."

This would be a big task, especially since it was likely that a substantial dowry had been paid on behalf of the daughter of such a rich man.

"What of your son-in-law? Will he agree?" I asked. Without such an agreement, it would be an even greater undertaking.

"Yes, or I'll break his neck myself and spare him the trouble of having his head chopped off in Jerusalem."

125

By the time Yosef finished with his lengthy story and the terms that he wanted in the bill of divorce, the sun had arced from east to west, and the booth was fully shaded. Nevertheless, Yosef's tunic under his robe was darkened in sweat. He had loosened the silk sash and opened his robe long ago. I filled my papyrus with scribbles, but these would be for my own use, the formal scribing of the bill would take great care, and I needed to consult with someone experienced in Torah, the Hebraic law. Would there be differences from the Roman law that I applied in Damascus? What was the effect of Torah in these uncertain times and in this Greco-Roman city? And, if the son-in-law was to agree as Yosef promised, I would need to meet with him to go over the document.

As I expected, the dowry for the daughter had been substantial, and much of the bill would be a recitation of the dowry items. The customary divorce would require a return of the dowry to the father of the bride. Since the dowry was now mixed with the household materials following the exodus from Arimathea, the bill of divorce would merely be a formal waiver of any future claims to the dowry. Most importantly, it would free the woman to remarry without the uncertainty of a husband lost in the fog of war. I judged that Yosef's primary concern was the dim prospect of heirs sired by a husband bound for demise in Jerusalem.

"The fool will die fighting the Romans," Yosef said.

"This irresponsible husband to my daughter will surely perish, but he calls me an old fool with false hopes. 'Yeshua of Nazareth was a high-minded dreamer,' he says. 'Yeshua was a worthy prophet,' he says, 'but he was not the mashiah.'"

With each stanza of his complaint, Yosef's tone grew shriller.

126

"'The mashiah will be a mighty conqueror,' he says, 'not a man who died feebly at the hands of the Romans.' He says, 'the true mashiah will crush the Romans.'"

And then his voice trailed off.

"'Yeshua is dead,' he says."

For a few moments, neither of us spoke before Yosef broke the silence.

"My father was there, you know," he said with a soft voice, not much more than a whisper.

"My father was part of the judicial council, the Sanhedrin, but he wasn't there for the hurry-up trial of Yeshua arranged by the High Priest in the middle of the night. There were plenty of right-thinking Pharisees who were upset following the connivance of the High Priest and Pontius Pilate," Yosef said, nodding his head for emphasis.

"Had there been a trial in the light of day ..." his voice trailed off, and he didn't finish his sentence. He was momentarily lost in a gaze toward the west and the hills of Judea. With a big sigh, he continued.

"My father provided the tomb for Yeshua's burial. Later, my father remained close to Ya'akov, the brother of Yeshua."

Questions bubbled up within me that I dared not ask of the rich man at this time and in this place. Perhaps one day.

"They had such great hopes, but my father is long dead, and Ya'akov himself was murdered by the High Priest."

Yosef nearly lost his composure, but he caught his emotions by covering his mouth with his hand, as if to trap the words that pained him. Enough had been spoken for this day. Yosef rose to his feet and nodded to his bodyguard, who stepped forward and counted out forty denarii. I

127

cupped both hands to receive the generous stipend. Yosef reminded me of a few details without looking at me. He started to walk away but then turned back.

He leaned close into my face. "They say I am an old fool who chases after ghosts. They say Yeshua was no mashiah, and he is long dead." Yosef's eyes glistened, and his voice cracked. "What do you say?"

Chapter Seventeen

I felt ill-prepared for drafting a bill of divorce for a Hebrew couple, initiated by the wife, with client expectations for a full return of the bridal dowry. When I asked Rafael, the synagogue leader, about Hebraic law regarding divorce, Rafael shrugged his shoulders and puffed out his lips.

"Who am I to judge? I am just an old wine merchant," and then he laughed. "We are not in Jerusalem, you know. We are in a free city of the Roman Empire. Roman law, not Torah, controls cases here in these lands."

I knew that the wife could initiate the divorce under Roman law, but what if the husband objected and claimed rights under Torah? My client promised it wouldn't turn messy and that the husband would agree to terms. Regardless of the law applied, I would scribe the bill of divorce in Greek: the language of contracts and commerce--even for the Aramaic-speaking Hebrews.

Just as I was leaving the synagogue, a throwaway remark by Rafael led to an unforeseen complication.

"Speak to the scribe that sits under the eucalyptus tree alongside the wadi outside the city," Rafael said. "I have heard that he knows of special rules that apply to the followers of Iesou."

I went straight from the synagogue. The season of the sun was upon us, and the winter rains that spilled runoff from the hills into a swollen wadi had ceased. The wadi would soon become a dry riverbed, but now occasional pools of stagnant water remained. I was pleased to find the scribe and a few produce merchants under the eucalyptus as promised. I tapped a few melons and purchased one that seemed ripe. This would be my gift to the scribe.

"Sit, sit," said the scribe with a gap-toothed grin that reached his ears.

He was an older man with patchy hair that peeked from beneath a linen headdress. He sat squat-legged on a goatskin rug wearing nothing but a loin cloth, and a long beard streaked with gray tickled his chest. He accepted the melon but cracked it open and handed one half back to me. Melon juice dribbled down our chins, into our beards, and sweetened our conversation. After I explained my purpose to the scribe, he bounded to his feet. He poured water into a basin and washed and dried his hands carefully before rummaging through a pile of goatskin bags.

"Yes, yes. Here, look at this." He extended a scroll toward me.

I also went to the wash basin before handling the scroll. I unrolled it and read the Greek script:

"Is it lawful for a man to divorce his wife?"

Iesou answered, "What did Moses command you?"

"Moses allowed a man to write a certificate of dismissal and to divorce her."

But Iesou said, "Because of your hardness of heart he wrote this commandment for you. But from the beginning of creation, 'God made them male and female.' 'For this reason, a man shall leave his father and mother and be joined to his wife, and the two shall become one flesh.' So, they are no longer two, but one flesh. Therefore, what God has joined together, let no one separate."

I was stunned; I was reading the words of Iesou, right there in front of me in black ink on a papyrus scroll, right there for anyone to read. I traced the words with a fingertip, as if by touching, I could hear the voice.

"Where did you get this scroll?"

"I scribed it myself."

The old scribe stood with one arm folded across his belly. The opposite arm crossed at right angles with his thumb cradling his chin and his forefinger tapping his nose, in a self-satisfied pose.

"I heard it spoken years ago at a synagogue in Galilee by someone who claimed he heard the words from Yeshua's own mouth, and I wrote it down because I knew I would need it when asked to write contracts of marriage or bills of divorce."

"May I copy it?"

The old scribe pursed his lips and rubbed his belly with both hands as if his thinking took place in his gut.

"Yes, I suppose. The scroll is mine but the words of Yeshua belong to many."

As I returned to the city along the wadi, a strange cloud hung in the western sky. The rumors were true; the dust of an army on the march darkened the setting sun, and the siege of Jerusalem had begun. The chaotic civil war left Jerusalem vulnerable to an empire that would not soon forget its humiliation at the hands of the Galilean insurgents just a few years earlier. I thought of the men in my command I had left behind, and I hoped--even as I knew better--that the city would make common cause to resist the Romans. *God's blessing be upon you, O Jerusalem, and all who huddle inside your walls awaiting what is sure to come--even you, Eleazar ben Simon.*

I did not sleep well as I worried about the bill of divorce and the words of Iesou, and I awoke with the dawn. I chewed on stale bread for my breakfast, but my water skins needed refilling, so I set out for the nearby fountain house. It was unusual to see others there so early, but half

131

a dozen Jewish men had gathered and spoke loudly with animated hand gestures.

"Have you heard? Did you hear?"

Several men competed to be the first to spill the news.

"Nero is dead! The emperor has swallowed poison!"

My mind raced as I filled my skins and listened to the wild speculation that bounced off the walls of the fountain house.

"The empire is finished!" said one, but that made no sense since violent death was the customary mode of imperial succession. It was rumored that Nero's own mother had poisoned her husband, Emperor Claudius, to elevate the sixteen-year-old Nero to the throne fourteen years earlier, and the imperial bodyguards, the Praetorians, had hacked Emperor Claudius to death before that.

"The legions will withdraw from Palestine to preserve order back in Rome!"

A hopeful thought, to be sure, but I doubted that imperial policy in the provinces would be much affected by the intrigues of Rome. A new emperor would soon claim the throne, and the provinces would continue to squirm under Roman hobnail boots. True enough, Nero had been the bitter enemy of the followers of Iesou, and he ordered the executions of Petros and Paulos and subjected the rest of the congregation in Rome to bitter persecution; a new emperor could do no worse.

"The new emperor will burn Jerusalem to the ground!" Scoffed one old man.

"No!"

"No!"

Hoots of derision drowned out the pessimist on this day for optimism, but I suspected cynicism was closest to the truth.

I spent the day idling and avoiding a meeting with my wealthy client. As the last flickers of sun slanted through the dust hanging in my stall, I packed my inks and papyrus sheets into my goatskin bag, tucked my reed pen behind my ear, and headed toward my lean-to quarters. I passed a gathering of young Jewish firebrands clustered around a tall jar filled with fresh brewed barley beer. I listened from the edge.

"The emperor is dead, and I say it was the hand of God," said a voice.

Another shouted. "Let us join the battle, God will smite our enemies."

I clanged on a tin pan with a spoon. "Listen to me; hear my words," I said as I climbed atop an ox cart, so all could see and hear me.

"The emperor is dead," I said. "It is true enough, but the siege army remains in place."

"Don't be a coward!" chimed a third voice.

Why is reason in the face of war-mongering always labeled as weakness?

"Let us join the brave men who defend the holy city," the voice continued. "Eleazar ben Simon is a great general, and God will lead him to victory!"

I had seen Eleazar face-to-face. He was a tyrant and a murderer but not a man of God. Nor were his co-conspirators and their dagger-men assassins nor the thugs they invited from Idumea. I witnessed the infighting and bloodletting as Jew killed Jew, and I knew the truth of it; Jerusalem was doomed.

The angry murmurings swelled. I again beat my tin pan with a spoon, but I had become invisible and irrelevant. How could I reason with the passions of young men soaked in barley beer? They ceased to listen, preferring to argue loudly with each other while keeping their cups full.

These young men who latched on to the reports of an emperor who swallowed hemlock, the refugees in the Nazarene camp, the city of Pella, the whole of Palestine--indeed, the entire cosmos--thirsted for good news, but I was convinced that death and destruction would greet the morrow. Yet … yet … was there was not more?

Chapter Eighteen

I could delay no longer; I requested an audience with my client, and a tall servant escorted me to Yosef's encampment along the roadway that led to the River Jordan. Gathering storm clouds across the river valley, hanging over the hills of the Galilee, obscured the sun. Lightning bulged from smoky clouds high in the heavens like the fires of a forge stoked by a bellows. I imagined thunder rolling from the Roman camps all the way south to Jerusalem. The storm clouds fit my mood as I carried bad news to my client. His daughter could not be divorced according to the command of Iesou.

The servant pulled back the flaps to the tent entrance and stepped aside with a gesture that encouraged me to step inside. As soon as I entered, a barrage of questions greeted me.

"Is the bill completed? Is there a problem? Why are you here?"

"Let the man sit," said a squat woman in silk robes that I assumed was Yosef's wife. "Bring fruit," she called to an unseen servant.

I joined Yosef, reclining on silk pillows, when a delicate young woman appeared with a clay dish brimming with slices of pears, cracked almonds, and yogurt. I momentarily forgot the serious business that brought me here, and the petite servant held my attention. She kept her eyes low as she leaned forward to hand the dish to me, but when her long hair, black as my inks, brushed across my extended hand, her nut-brown cheeks flushed a soft pink, and her moist, green eyes darted into mine as she mouthed "sorry." My eyes followed the servant girl and Yosef's wife as they disappeared into unseen recesses of the vast tent.

"What news?" Yosef asked.

I presumed he inquired about the bill of divorce and not political gossip from Rome, and I pulled the scroll from my goatskin bag.

"May I read this to you?"

Yosef nodded, and I read the words of Iesou copied from the old scribe's scroll.

"What does this mean?" Yosef asked. The old man's olive-skinned face blanched. "Does Iesou overrule Moses?"

I was momentarily set off my task by Yosef's simple question. Who could overrule the Law of Moses, Torah itself, the essence of Hebrew society and self-understanding? Before I could think through the implications of Yosef's innocent insight, Yosef's pleading voice brought me back to the immediate problem.

"Please, there must be a way around this hurdle," Yosef said. "Hava must be granted a divorce."

"But, in the new reign which Iesou proclaims, there will be no divorce," I said.

"What new reign is that?" Yosef did not ask a question but made a statement. "As I look toward Jerusalem, all I see is smoke. No kingdom is visible."

I did not reply. For the first time, I took a sip from my wine cup. The parables of the tale teller filled my mind. *The reign of God is like a mustard seed*, the tale teller had intoned in his sing-song voice. Nearly every parable recited by the tale teller began the same way, *the reign of God is like ...* I knew well from the parables and stories I had gathered that Iesou's preaching and teaching centered on the coming reign of God ... the kingdom of God ... the dominion of God ... but what was his meaning?

136

"The ink strokes on your scroll speak of the beginning of creation, the garden of Eden, paradise, perfection," Yosef said. "Is a return to the garden of Eden the coming reign of God that Yeshua proclaims?"

Yosef gulped down his cup of wine and poured another. "This rebellious husband chooses to separate himself from his wife and the community. Instead of Eden, he chooses to go down to Sheol."

I said nothing as Yosef ranted with hard questions that I couldn't answer, but perhaps he saw a way forward with the pressing issue at hand, the matter of the divorce. Were Iesou's words command or promise? Did Iesou prohibit divorce here and now or was he merely anticipating the idyllic reign of God in which broken relationships would be no more? Was this new rule for all of humankind or just the community? If it was just the community, Yosef had correctly pointed out that the rebellious husband was about to divorce himself from the community so could Hava not divorce him?

Yosef drained his wine cup again and refilled it. The color was returning to his face.

"It is not a legal question," I suggested, thinking out loud. "According to Hebrew law and Roman law, the divorce will be permitted and recognized ... if you choose to proceed despite the words of Iesou."

Yosef nodded his head.

"So, you will scribe a bill of divorce if I ask?"

Yosef leaned forward and filled my wine cup to the brim.

"Yes," I said with a shrug of my shoulders.

It would take several days for me to complete the bill of divorce: a copy in black ink for Yosef and Hava and a copy in red ink for the

137

husband. Our business was done for this evening, and I jammed the reed pen behind my ear lobe.

But I didn't leave immediately, and wineskins of well-aged wine were emptied--too many to count. Plates of meats and fishes and cheeses appeared then disappeared. Each time the curtain parted, I glanced quickly to see if the beautiful servant girl returned, but she never did.

If I hadn't drunk three or four cups of wine, I probably wouldn't have said anything, but I just blurted it out. I'm not sure why, but it seemed I ate and drank with the old Nazarene on false pretenses.

"I'm not circumcised."

Yosef suddenly seemed wide awake; he stared long and hard, weighing what I had just said. He bit off a chunk of hard cheese and chewed on it a long time before he swallowed. Finally, his bushy eyebrows twitched, and he said,

"As you say, this is a new day, and we have left the old behind, and we travel to a new land, the land of the Gentiles. Praise be to God!"

It seemed we had struck an odd friendship; certainly, the solution to Hava's divorce problem was a big part of it, but there was more. Perhaps it stemmed from the hope we heard in the written words of Iesou that made him present, alive still: speaking, teaching, and leading. The good news was implicit … the beginning of creation. The world was turning. For us, Iesou was pointing forward not back. Iesou announced a new rule, a new relationship, and a new ideal for a new day in a new reign. Jerusalem truly was writhing in death throes, but it was the old order making way for the new; it was not the end but the beginning. The time is fulfilled, and the reign of God has come near.

138

Iesou had issued a new word--beyond Moses, beyond Torah, more stringent than Torah--for a new day. A new teaching—with authority! Iesou was a Torah teacher, but he was more. He was a prophet, but he was more. He was the mashiah, but not as the people expected. The foolish son-in-law would run off to fight for Jerusalem, but he misunderstood. The false mashiahs from the Galilee misunderstood. Jerusalem misunderstood. Even the disciples had misunderstood.

It was well into the second watch of the night when Yosef's servants finally escorted me to my quarters near my stall in the marketplace.

Four days later, I returned to the tent camp of Yosef with a freshly scribed bill of divorce. First, I huddled with Yosef alone, and I read the bill to him slowly with many interruptions for discussion. I pulled my reed pen from its characteristic place behind my ear and traced the ink strokes on the papyrus as I read. Yosef was not a learned man, and he could not read the document himself, so he depended upon my careful reading and explanation. That was what scribes were for.

"I'm satisfied. You made it right, and even more. Well done, my young friend," Yosef said, and he patted me on the back.

Next came the son-in-law, Abner. A servant departed and returned with a tall man with dark, curly locks over a furrowed brow.

"May we speak alone," Abner said to me with a nervous glance at Yosef.

I looked at Yosef and said, "It's a fair request."

Yosef looked at the son-in-law, then at me with probing eyes that said he was taking my measure. Quickly, a smile settled on Yosef's face.

"Yes, go ahead. I'm sure you can handle it," Yosef said.

I was pleased at the show of support.

When Yosef departed, Abner barely glanced at the document.

"I'm sure it is in good order," he said as he signed the document before he rolled the papyrus sheet into a scroll. "I owe a great deal to Yosef, and I deeply regret the offense I have caused." His eyes welled, and he turned away from me. He tapped the scroll against the side of his head and then tossed it onto a table. "And Hava is a sweet young thing ..."

He cleared his throat. "But I must fight for mother Jerusalem. The cause may be hopeless, I know that, but I am a Jew and I must fight with my people, and if that means dying alongside my brothers, well, praise be to God. I wish Yosef understood that."

"Why am I ranting to you? A Gentile wouldn't understand."

I didn't correct him. My father had been Jewish, but I was not circumcised so perhaps I was a Gentile and not a Jew. Could there not be a mixture?

"What I don't understand is why Yosef and these accursed followers of Yeshua abandon mother Jerusalem."

I breathed deeply but said nothing; as the scribe handling the man's divorce, it would be improper decorum to disagree.

"A dead man, humiliated on the cross without so much as a fight," he said, shaking his head, "is no mashiah, and only fools--or cowards--would forsake Jerusalem to follow a ghost."

Abner paused, drawing deep breaths and running his fingers through his hair. After a few moments, he concluded his comments in a soft voice.

"Who am I to know? Yosef has made his choice, and I have made mine. May God have mercy on each of us."

He stomped out of the tent. He didn't bother taking his copy of the bill of divorce.

140

I remained alone for quite a while, and I began to wonder if I should go looking for Yosef. I stepped to the tent door, and I witnessed the parting of Yosef and his now former son-in-law. Others were there as well. I recognized several of the foolish young firebrands from the marketplace. Yosef handed him a sack, undoubtedly filled with coins, and then Yosef instinctively extended his hand. When Abner mounted a piebald gelding, Yosef slapped it on its rear, and Abner and the others galloped away.

When Yosef returned to the tent, he clapped his hands and bellowed, "Hava. It is done. Come!"

I gathered my inks and carefully packed them into my goat-leather bag, sticking the reed pen behind my ear. When I finished, I turned to await the arrival of the daughter, Hava, but I was surprised to find her standing quietly behind me. I opened my mouth to greet her, but the words caught in my throat. The beautiful servant girl was no servant; she was the daughter.

After an awkward silence, Yosef spoke. "Is something wrong? Come sit and let us do our business."

The daughter and I moved to sitting positions on pillows with Yosef between us.

I extended the document toward her, but then quickly withdrew it.

"I suppose I should read this to you."

"You may read it to me if you like, but I'm comfortable reading it myself."

Yosef's smug smile and a sparkle in his eyes said he was proud he had allowed an educated daughter. I hesitated briefly then passed the document to Hava. Yosef and I remained silent while she read the bill; a couple of times she drew a deep breath and appeared to be on the verge of

141

speaking, but she said nothing. I couldn't read her emotions. Was she pleased at the divorce? Did she love her husband? I felt oddly jealous at the thought.

"So be it," she said and lightly rose to her feet, and I scrambled to my feet as well.

Facing me, she bowed slightly with a forced smile. "Thank you."

She also nodded politely toward her father then quickly exited the room. Yosef knit his eyebrows and strained his beard through his fingers as he watched her leave. He turned his gaze to me with an expression that said he was sizing me up in a new light. With a nod of the head and a harrumph under his breath, he smiled.

Chapter Nineteen

The summer months passed hot and dry, and the ears of corn, the grains of wheat, and the oat stalks shriveled. Granary stocks dwindled as drought visited the hills and valleys of Pella. The old men of the city said they had never seen such scarcity in their lifetimes. Thus, when the synagogue celebrated the autumnal harvest festival known as *Sukkot*, famine heightened the urgency to seek divine favor.

When I ascended the steps of the Pella synagogue and passed through the pillars and across the portico, I expected to join a community united in need and in hope. I didn't anticipate a riot.

I squeezed into a seat on the upper row of benches along the side of the hall. I recognized a few Nazarene faces and a few Jewish vendors from the market, but mostly the benches were filled with strangers. I felt conspicuous and naked because I wore no prayer shawl with ritual fringes as did so many of those gathered.

Across the hall, my eyes fell upon Mishael and Anina with Mattithyahu seated between them. The recently divorced Hava and her father sat next to them. The two women leaned in for conversation punctuated by laughter. Anina spotted me and waved; the women giggled, and I felt my face flush.

A quavering, extended blast on a ram's horn, a *shofar*, signaled the beginning of the processional. The assembly hushed as Rabbi Rafael processed in with attendants following with scrolls of Torah and the prophets. Other attendants carried willow branches, and children followed with a clump of branches bound together with a palm frond. The procession circled the Torah shrine seven times, and then the willow branches were placed around the shrine where other willow branches had already been affixed. The children tittered and squatted on the tile floor.

"Blessed be the Lord forever," Rafael intoned, and the liturgy began.

First came the *Shema*: Hear O Israel, the Lord is our God, the Lord is One ... Most of the Jews closed their eyes and fingered the fringes on their prayer shawls as they recited the familiar words in sing-song fashion.

Then came the *Tefillah*, and the congregation rose to its feet for the multi-stanza prayer. When Rafael concluded the prayers with the blessing first offered by Aaron to the Israelites in the wilderness--*The Lord bless you and keep you; the Lord make his face to shine upon you and be gracious to you; the Lord lift up his countenance upon you and give you peace*--the congregation sat down.

An attendant handed Rafael a scroll, and he carefully unfurled it until he reached the appointed passage, and then he set the scroll upon the shrine.

"Hear the words of Zechariah the prophet," Rafael said, and he began to read from a text frequently used as *Sukkot* liturgy.

I will gather all the nations against Jerusalem to battle, and the city shall be taken, and the houses looted, and the women raped; half the city shall go into exile, but the rest of the people shall not be cut off from the city.

At first, it was striking that the words of old seemed to be coming true in our time, but then, the promises grew cold and cruel in their lack of fulfillment.

Then the Lord will go forth and fight against those nations as when he fights on a day of battle ... This shall be the plague with which the Lord will strike all the peoples that wage war against Jerusalem: their flesh

144

shall rot while they are still on their feet; their eyes shall rot in their
sockets, and their tongues shall rot in their mouths ... And a plague like
this plague shall fall on the horses, the mules, the camels, the donkeys, and
whatever animals may be in those camps.

My head swirled. Such boasts, such promises, such ... rot! How can
we trust the prophet when we see the dust of the siege armies across the
Jordan? It would seem the decay is not in the tongues of the enemy but in
the beguiling words of the prophet. With Jerusalem facing annihilation,
divine intervention seemed not a promise but a taunt.

"Hear the words of Moses," Rafael continued, and then he began a
second traditional *Sukkot* reading from the Deuteronomy scroll:

If you will only heed his every commandment that I am commanding
you today—loving the Lord your God, and serving him with all your heart
and with all your soul—then he will give the rain for your land in its
season, the early rain and the later rain, and you will gather in your grain,
your wine, and your oil; and he will give grass in your fields for your
livestock, and you will eat your fill. Take care, or you will be seduced into
turning away, serving other gods and worshiping them, for then the anger
of the Lord will be kindled against you and he will shut up the heavens, so
that there will be no rain and the land will yield no fruit; then you will
perish quickly off the good land that the Lord is giving you.

When the rabbi finished, he gingerly rolled up the scroll and handed it
back to the attendant. He sat down, and others rose to speak.

The first speaker extolled the promise of Jerusalem. Yes, Jerusalem
was threatened now--he admitted--but the Lord's Day was nigh--the
speaker promised--and God's plague would rot the Legions in their place,

145

and Rome and all the Gentile nations would one day soon bring rich sacrifice to the altars of the victorious God of Israel.

The assembly filled with whispers when Symeon, the Nazarene from Jerusalem, the head of the twelve, stepped forward into the center of the hall. He held out an open palm and lifted his face toward the ceiling.

"Where is the rain?"

The stout man lowered his gaze and scanned the congregation. His face feigned puzzlement.

"Where is the grain, the wine, the oil?" He extended both hands to emphasize his perplexing questions. Symeon had a naturally deep voice, and his growled interrogation grew louder, "Where is the grass in the fields? Why is the livestock mere skin and bones?"

He paused to let his questions sink in. Certainly, this congregation and community had been asking the same questions as drought parched the fields and withered the fruit on the vine. Then, suddenly he bellowed.

"Are we not seduced? Have we not turned away? Are we not serving other gods and worshiping them? Is not the Lord's anger kindled against us, and has he not shut up the heavens?"

By the end of Symeon's sermon in the form of an interrogation, his voice boomed off the hewn-stone walls. He had masterfully spun the words of Moses into a seductive web, and then the spider pounced. His voice dropped to a whisper, and the congregation leaned in.

"Yeshua is the one," he said, and the congregation was jolted. "Yeshua is the anointed of God. He who was crucified will return to lead God's army and deliver God's people, and we, you and I, invite God's wrath through our unbelief." With voice rising over swelling murmurs, he concluded, "Where is the rain?"

146

Lord, have mercy. Lord, forgive my apostasy, for I doubt. The Jews are fools, but are the Nazarenes any better? They are so bound to the old way of thinking that when a new thing happens in their midst, they cannot see it. Symeon the cousin, the twelve, and all the twelves before them were setting their minds on human things and not on divine things. "Who do you say that I am"--that is certainly the question, but Iesou is no warrior-king, he is no mashiah in the manner expected by the tradition or the Nazarenes. Lord have mercy.

The congregation stirred uneasily, and unfriendly grousing swelled up. This was not a new boast from the Nazarenes. The congregation had heard this claim before. In the early days, some even dared hope it was true, but then the man had been crucified, the years passed, and now Jerusalem's enemies choked her by the throat, and where was Yeshua? Dead and buried.

"Blasphemy!"

"You defile this holy place!"

"It is you who cause the heavens to dry up!"

When angry congregants began to move toward Symeon, Rafael struggled to restore order.

"Please, please, return to your seats. Return to your seats, now, and we shall pray."

The crowd paid no heed, and angry shouts crescendoed. I ploughed through the mob straightaway to Hava and Yosef on the opposite side.

"Come, we must leave here," I said, and I cradled Hava with my right arm around her waist and cleared a pathway with my left. Yosef trailed behind. Mishael followed Yosef, clutching Mattithyahu close to his chest, and Anina grasped his robe and followed along.

I slept in fits that night, and the events of the day bounced around in my head as I squirmed on my goatskin mat, alone in the dark. I rose and scooped a cup of water from a vase then stepped outside my hut and gazed at the heavens. Black clouds scudded past a distant moon. I shivered, and my breath fogged around my face. I drained my cup and returned to my mat, wrapped in another goatskin for warmth. Winter was on my doorstep.

As sleep neared, a woman crept into my thoughts. When I had drawn Yosef's daughter in close to protect her as we scurried out of the synagogue, I remembered what I had forgotten: the touch of a woman. When I finally drifted off to sleep, the softness, the fragrance, and the sweet voice of Hava filled my dreams.

Chapter Twenty

Winter arrived on a single day. Sullen clouds and a grim mist settled into the Pella valley as I walked to my lean-to stall after filling my waterskins at the nearby fountain house. I pulled my hood over my skull cap and trudged forward with head bowed and one hand clutching my robe under my chin. As morning became midday, an angry breeze pelted my stall with raindrops and forced me to stow my papyrus and inks in my goatskin bag, and I eased back into a protected corner of my nook and chewed on hard bread. Across the alley, a single raven swayed on a branch of a dead willow. The breeze ruffled the bird's tar-colored feathers and tossed the branch until it snapped. With a single caw, the raven disappeared into the drizzle.

Did I hear a far-off shout? Did the fickle wind deceive me? I canted my head, and my ears heard garbled snatches. I tossed back my hooded robe and stepped to the edge of my stall as a lone boy materialized out of the mist. He ran barefoot, bareheaded, and barely dressed save for a loincloth, yet he seemed oblivious to the wind and rain as he jogged through the puddles. His face turned this way and that to shout at the curious who stepped into the weather at his approach. As he neared my stall, his glare captured my wondering eyes. As he passed by, he bellowed the horrible rumor once more.

"There has been a killing in the Nazarene settlement! A Nazarene woman has been raped and murdered!"

I took off running. When I shed a sandal, I kept running. When I splashed through a muddy wadi, I stumbled and rolled but came up running. When I reached the grassy slope of the settlement, I saw a cluster of folks gathered around a tent; I knew the tent, and my heart sagged.

I burst into the mix of angry men, weeping women, and wailing children. I grabbed the first woman I came to with my hands on her quaking shoulders; she sobbed uncontrollably. I moved to the next. I probed her eyes, and I saw the terrible truth. It was Anina. The granddaughter of Ya'akov. The grandniece of Iesou. Anina was their favorite, their princess, the flesh and blood heir of their king. Not Anina. Sweet, gentle, kind Anina. My tears flowed along with the others. My shoulders heaved with sobs.

Often, the greatest crimes make the least sense and the greatest criminals are the least of men. Within hours, the murderer was captured, and Cyrus and the other magistrates ordered the execution of a known thug, born of a local prostitute, a petty thief and idler. He confessed no motive, no reason, no purpose for the evil he unleashed.

The magistrates allowed the execution to proceed according to Hebrew custom; the killer would be stoned to death by the Nazarene community. A gully was hollowed out and dug to twice the height of a man. Rocks were arranged to line the bottom. Bound at the wrists, the killer was led to the edge, and Mishael, the aggrieved husband, pushed the man into the pit and onto the rocks. He was injured but alive, laying on his back atop the stones. Once again, it was the duty of Mishael to toss the first stone, a heavy slab that landed on the killer's chest, but still he remained alive, writhing with choking breaths and bloody spittle at the bottom of the pit. Now it became the responsibility of the community to continue with the stoning, and I did my duty; I was numb as I picked up a rock the size a melon and heaved it, but loosing the stone did nothing to appease my anguish.

At the edge of the massed onlookers, a mother wailed as her son died; she wept alone, and no one comforted her.

Justice was done, and the murderer paid for his crime, but the wounds to the souls of the Nazarenes were not healed. What shocked the Nazarenes was that the murderer was Jewish, born of the blood of Abraham. And where was God? Was He cruel in causing this death or merely heartless in allowing it to happen?

As the sun ebbed in the west, I returned to my lean-to and drained a wineskin, so quickly that the bitter liquid slobbered around my mouth and dripped into my beard, but my thirst was not quenched. I slung three empty skins over my shoulder and hurried to a nearby wine merchant, hoping that he would open his shop to me even though the hour was late.

"But I sup with my family," the vendor said when I pounded on his door. "Come back in the morn."

"An extra denarius for you," I said, offering a full day's wage.

"Would you pay two?"

"Done," I said and followed the man to an anteroom where the back wall was lined with tall vases.

After he filled the first skin, I drank from it while he filled the second and third skins.

"More," I said and handed the half-empty skin back to the man, who clucked his disapproval but topped off the skin anyway.

I stepped into the night, but I had lost my bearings, and I wasn't sure which way to turn.

"Where are you?"

I stepped forward, but God was not there; I went backward but I could not find him.

151

"Do you hide to the left?" I turned too quickly and wrenched the knee that had long been healed, and I stumbled.

I sat for a moment and a few swallows, before I awkwardly regained my feet against the protests of my screaming knee.

"Do you conceal yourself to my right?"

I staggered in that direction, but I soon found myself in a woodlot on the edge of the city, where thick darkness engulfed me. I surrendered to the pleas of my knee to sit, and I must have dozed off until raindrops splashed against my face, but I slipped in the mud as I attempted to stand. I groveled in the muck with the worms, but I managed to regain my feet and find my way back to my lean-to. I had lost one wineskin. Only one full skin left.

I took a couple of swallows as I searched for my dagger. I spilled my sack of writing implements, but the *pugio* wasn't there. I drank more wine. I looked under my mat and found the knife. I fingered the blade, testing for sharpness but nicked my thumb. I licked the blood and chased it with the dregs from the last wineskin, which I threw against the wall.

We must decide if creation is good or evil and act accordingly.

She said it, and I believed it, but now my decision was different. There is no justice, save what we do ourselves. An eye for an eye. Evil returns evil. I strapped the sheath onto my hip and headed into the night, stumbling and falling often. Each time I fell, it seemed I landed on my knee that howled in judgment. I wandered the backstreets searching for the hut that served as brothel. When I arrived, I pushed the heavy door open to find three women inside, but not the one I sought.

"Come in. Come in honey."

"Where is she?" I demanded.

152

"Surely one of us will do," said the oldest with drooping red-stained cheeks that had faded to pink. She dug beneath my sash and pulled out my purse which burst open, spilling coins onto the dusty floor.

"Oh honey, you have enough for all three of us."

Her hands probed deeper beneath my tunic. The second whore scrounged for coins on the floor while the third opened her robe and rubbed her bare breasts in my face.

"Ooh, don't bite," she said and slapped me and giggled.

The sun broke through the square hole of a window high atop the opposite wall and lit up the mat where I lay on my back, stark naked. I took a deep breath, rubbed my eyes, and shook my thick head. For a few seconds, I leaned on my elbows, but the room lurched around me, and I laid back down. I gulped big breaths trying to speed the process of coming alive. Finally, I sat up feeling for my clothes.

"Looking for this?" A voice came from the shadows in the corner as my tunic hit me in the face.

I quickly dressed and covered myself. A woman in a hood stepped forward with her back to the sun and her shadowed face toward me.

"Did you come for me? Well, here I am. You may rape me if that is your purpose."

I squinted as I tried to make her out.

"Did you come to beat me? Go ahead, pummel me with your fists."

I stepped back and shielded my eyes from the sun that haloed around her hood.

"If you came to cut me, take up your dagger, and do what you must."

She tossed my *pugio*, and it landed point down and quivered in the dirt floor near my feet.

"Or, did you come to kill the mother of the killer?"

The woman threw back her hood and ripped her robe open, exposing her chest.

"Then claim your justice; cut my heart out."

I retreated until my back hit the wall behind me. I attempted to speak, but my voice barely squeaked.

"Have you come to console me?" The woman said in a mocking tone. She returned to her three-legged stool in the corner and sobbed quietly. "Don't waste your pity on me. I am inconsolable."

I cleared my throat and again attempted to speak, but she cut me off.

"Don't you dare forgive me! My shame is all that remains that I may call my own. Please don't steal it from me."

The door across the room opened, and I bolted out. A few days later when I arrived at my workplace stall, I found my *pugio* wrapped carefully in its sheath and my purse with the coins replenished.

The death of one was nearly the death of all. The knife at the throat of the Nazarene community was fear--not just fear of the Romans or of the Jews--but existential fear, the threat of chaos, and despondency was a more present danger than annihilation. Anina's murder inaugurated a season of discontent: a winter of recurrent rain, wind, and cold that chilled the face and numbed the soul. The leaden clouds that blanketed the Pella valley threatened suffocation.

The Nazarenes never returned to the Pella synagogue. Many abandoned prayers altogether and shuffled along, one meaningless step after another. Others chose a path of rigidity and scrupulosity. God's abandonment could only mean that the people had failed him. Mishael, Anina's widower, was one of these.

Mishael said little as the days turned into weeks. He held his grief close--too close, said the Nazarene women who fed him with pots of stew and loaves of bread, who washed his clothes, and who invited his son to play, but he was reluctant to separate himself from young Mattithyahu. By midwinter, his grief began to seep out as free-floating anger that attached itself to whatever was near. He snapped at the women who ministered to him, he argued with vendors in the market, he brought trivial complaints to the magistrates, and he railed against the enemies left behind in Jerusalem: unbelieving Jews, murdering Romans, dishonest Sadducees, and a priesthood that did not know God.

Eventually, his anger focused. Gentiles became his fixation, especially those Gentile usurpers who claimed to follow Yeshua but who polluted the purity of his memory and his cause. Though it had been a Jewish thug who murdered his wife, he indirectly blamed the Gentile interlopers. He was a leader of the Nazarenes, and God had punished him for failing to mind God's holy law. No mixing and mingling—was that not the essence of Torah boundaries? The vine grower must not sow his vineyard with a second kind of seed; the farmer must not plow with an ox and a donkey yoked together; the warp of the weaver must not be wool if the woof was linen. God's people must distinguish between the holy and the common, the clean and the unclean.

Most importantly, no mixing of Gentile and Jew. Why had the mashiah not returned? Why had his own dear wife been murdered? Mishael saw it clearly now, and he would be lax no longer. He spoke only

155

Aramaic, and he refused to acknowledge any person who spoke to him in Greek. He regularized his prayer schedule, and he became fastidious in his ritual washings and scrupulous with his tithes.

If Mishael responded to his wife's murder with religious scrupulosity, my reaction was merely gloomy pessimism. Each day, I arrived late to my stall. There was little work, and I had little ambition for the few tasks my occupation assigned to me. The raven that had been the omen of Anina's death mocked me throughout the dreary winter. The bird's beady-eyes taunted me from a perch in the dead branches of the willow tree across the alley. Whenever I became preoccupied with work, a raspy caw would issue from the bird's black throat as if to say, "Pay attention to me. Don't ignore your melancholy." I flung rocks at the bird, but it would merely lift off and alight again.

My own anger was also free-floating. The murderous rage I initially felt toward the prostitute had nowhere else to settle, so I went back to blaming God. And then I was angry with myself for having trusted God. And then one day I realized I was angry with Anina, for she had led me away from my earlier melancholy toward hoping and believing that life had meaning, that I had value, and that I had a purpose. She had been the trickster, and I was her fool. I had loved her dearly--not as a man loves a woman--but as kindred souls on a journey of the spirit to a mysterious but glorious destination. That was the false hope she had engendered in me, but then she was gone, and I was left alone with no path to follow.

Many years ago, I read a letter to my mother, a letter from her dear friend Paulos the apostle, who wrote, "Where, O death, is your victory? Where, O death, is your sting?" The raven that taunted me from the perch on the dead willow branch put the lie to the optimism of the man from Tarsos.

Chapter Twenty-one

Begging was an honorable profession for the blind and lame, and a backstreet of Pella known as "Beggars Row" included many of these. And one former prostitute who sat alone, because men would no longer share the bed of the mother of a demon, and even the beggars ostracized her. Snowflakes flecked her gray-streaked, disheveled black hair, and she shivered in a threadbare robe.

She sat silent and ignored but bolted upright as if awakened from slumber when I dropped a copper coin in the empty plate near her red and raw bare feet.

"You!" she said, and her eyes bulged as they followed me down the street.

I went straightaway to the tents of Yosef, but it was Hava who greeted me.

"May I have a few woman's garments, old and used will do, but warm and hardy?" I asked.

Hava canted her head and raised her eyebrows.

"What?"

I repeated my request, and Hava's curiosity only increased.

"Why? For whom?"

"For an old beggar woman."

Hava disappeared into the folds of the tent and returned after a few minutes with a thick bundle wrapped in a woolen cloak.

"Tell me more, Scribe, why do you worry about this old woman."

"It is she."

Her mouth dropped, and eyes widened.

"Why her?"

"Because she is cold."

Hava gave me a look I had not seen before.

"Wait, and I shall go with you."

She disappeared momentarily and returned dressed warmly in her own woolen cloak with a hood, clutching a basket of bread and cheeses.

"What is your name?" I asked when we arrived back at Beggar's Row.

The woman was wary but didn't hesitate to wolf down the bread, and she spoke through a mouthful.

"I don't have a name, or if I do, I don't remember," she said, and she grabbed a chunk of cheese.

"What shall we call you?"

"Call me what you will. No, wait. Call me Rahab."

For the first time, there was a glimmer in her eyes at her own joke, naming herself after the Jericho prostitute of legend, who helped secure the promised land for the Israelites.

Hava draped the cloak over the woman's shoulders. At first, Rahab recoiled but then grasped Hava's hand.

"What is your name, dearie?"

"I am Hava."

Rahab took a long drink of water from the skin we brought, then silently ruminated on her bread for a few moments, staring in the direction of the theater and the encampment beyond.

"Tell me about the woman who died," she said without looking at either of us.

Spring crept in with little fanfare. It simply arrived, and the great festival of spring, the Passover, seemed merely another waypoint on the road to nowhere. With evening darkness settling on Pella, the annual *Seder* began on the 14th day of Nisan, the month of spring and of miracles. I was invited to eat the *Seder* with the household of Yosef ben Yosef. The *Seder* meal, the ritual reenactment of God's salvation in rescuing his people Israel from captivity in Egypt centuries earlier, was the highpoint of the festival of Passover.

My thoughts wandered as I drank the first cup of red wine, commemorative of the blood spilled in Egypt and in circumcision. Yosef recited the familiar story of the exodus from Egypt. More than ever, I didn't feel that these rituals were my own.

A reading of a praise passage from the psalmist preceded the second cup, and then the meal began: vegetables as an appetizer, the breaking of the unleavened matzah, bitter herbs to finish. Perhaps it was the wine that raised my spirits or perhaps it was the laugh in the voice of Hava and the smile on her face. The occasional meals taken that dark winter in the tents of Yosef and in the company of his wife and daughter had been rare oases of light.

By the third cup, my thoughts carried me home to Damascus where the Iesou community had adopted new rituals, new remembrances, and new promises for the *Seder* centered not in the exodus from Egypt but on Iesou and his blood and his passion. The Damascus community had learned the celebration of Iesou's last supper from the Antioch community and Paulos the apostle. Recently, I spoke often of Damascus to Yosef and his family, and Hava's questions about my homeland encouraged me to remember and share.

After the fourth cup of wine, I surprised myself by daring to speak what had been on my mind.

"We should depart Pella and take refuge in Damascus," I said.

"We?" asked Hava.

I departed early the next morning for the short walk to my stall. The sun shone brightly in a cloudless sky, and the breeze warmed my face. As I swung my goatskin bag from my shoulder, I spied something under the dead willow. As I crossed the alley to see what I had seen, I noticed that the raven was not perched in the tree. I knelt and brushed away a clump of dead leaves from the green shoot that poked through the humus.

The Caravan 69 CE

Now the LORD said to Abram, "Go from your country and your kindred and your father's house to the land that I will show you. I will make of you a great nation, and I will bless you, and make your name great, so that you will be a blessing. I will bless those who bless you, and the one who curses you I will curse; and in you all the families of the earth shall be blessed."

Genesis 12:1-3

I will lead the blind by a road they do not know, by paths they have not known I will guide them. I will turn the darkness before them into light, the rough places into level ground.

Isaiah 42:16

Chapter Twenty-two

I was not alone in my desire to depart Pella, and plans for a caravan to head north swirled about with anticipation; some would journey as far as Damascus, and others would continue to Antioch. Mishael the widower and his son had already departed for Antioch a month earlier. Not all would leave, and Symeon would remain as leader of the Nazarene remnant that planned to return to Jerusalem once the war had run its course. Yosef and his extensive household would form the core of the caravan. Transporting Yosef's livestock and possessions would be a massive undertaking, and Yosef was too old to do it alone.

"Who am I to lead a caravan?" I protested when Yosef suggested that I serve as overseer. "I am a mere scribe. You want me to write a contract? I'll do it. You want me to list your inventory? I'll do it. You want me to scribe a bill of sale? I'll do it. But lead a caravan? I've never been astride a camel. I find them foul smelling and ill tempered."

Yosef and others encouraged and persisted until I relented. Jews were scapegoats these days, and it would be best if a Greek-speaking overseer from Damascus led the caravan.

In preparation, I rode with Yosef on horseback to the ruins of the Greek fort atop the highest hill a mile away. From there, we could see the lay of the land and plan our journey. Once again, I gazed upon Mt. Hermon in the haze far to the north. Earlier, the panorama touched my melancholy and uncertainty, but today, Mt. Hermon invited me home.

As our mounts trotted down the trail back toward Pella, we came across a riderless horse grazing in the undulating grasses. Yosef's daughter, Hava, was there on the hillside picking flowers.

"Silly woman," said Yosef. "Will you stay and mind that she returns safely?"

Yosef trotted off, and I dismounted and allowed my horse to join the other that munched contentedly.

"These are for you," Hava teased when I approached.

She extended a bouquet of yellow marigolds mixed with blood-red windflowers. Not knowing what else to do, I accepted them. She plucked a groundsel and slowly blew the white hairs away. Each hair bore a seed that the wind carried where it would.

"We'll depart soon for Damascus," I said.

"I know," she said. "Papa tells me you will be the caravan master."

Just then, the breeze swirled, and I felt a chill. Storm clouds gathered in the west.

"It will soon rain," I said. "We better head back."

"If you say so, Master," she teased.

I found her mildly vexing, but I didn't know how to respond. As she mounted her horse, I awkwardly extended my hand for assistance, but she ignored me.

"Catch me if you can," Hava said, and her bay mare broke into a gallop.

I was familiar enough with riding a horse, but I was not a horseman, and Hava quickly outdistanced me. Unlike many women, she didn't sit her horse gingerly. She leaned forward, aligning herself with the neck and guided the mare with her knees, not her hands. I bounced about, but Hava's motions were at one with her mount; many hours together had earned mutual trust between horse and rider. I lost sight of her, and when I reached the encampment, she was already there rubbing down her mare.

I was greeted with a wry smile.

The column stretched over many cubits. As the overseer, I sat astride my horse by the side of the road as the caravan--camels and horses with riders; donkeys laden with goods; livestock including goats, sheep, and a few cattle and oxen pulling wagons; and a motley mix of foot travelers--crept by. One of these was Rahab the prostitute who pleaded with me earlier.

"Please take me with you," she said.

"Of course," I replied.

It seemed I had become her protector and Hava her benefactor. She appeared healthy and fit, thanks to the regular food she received from Hava. I guessed her to be a generation older than me, but the years of her hard life may have made her appear older than she was.

At the rear were the hangers-on who benefited from the security of the host. It seemed my shadow moved faster than the single-file procession. A single rider on horseback would travel the seventy odd miles to Damascus in two days--three at the most, but Yosef and I planned to spend a fortnight, maybe more, covering the same ground. Transporting Yosef's tent complex, livestock, and household would be a major migration.

We chose the eastern road to Damascus to avoid the concentrations of Roman legionaries around the Sea of Galilee, including the Roman enclave at Caesarea Philippi that dominated the western slopes of Mt. Hermon and the northern hills of the Galilee. The rebellion started in the Galilee, and that is where the Romans exacted harsh revenge. Entire Jewish villages were annihilated by the Romans, and the smoke from burnt out ruins and the stink of corpses rotting on crosses wafted throughout the Galilean countryside. Better to risk the rigors of arid lands than to encounter hostile Roman legionaries. Our route would take us along the shifting edge of the Nabatean kingdom of the Arabs that scraped against the Roman Empire.

After following the Jordan River north for a short distance, we would branch off at the mouth of the Yarmuk River where it flowed into the Jordan just south of the Sea of Galilee. We would cross over the Yarmuk near the river's mouth and follow the trail along the northern banks of the river as it twisted east. After several day's journey along the Yarmuk, we would turn north to cross the high plateau that skirted the Syrian Desert. The closer we would get to Damascus, the more inhospitable the terrain, especially considering our livestock.

We would not be alone. It was normal for travelers to bunch with a caravan for protection, and with each passing day, the tail of our column stretched farther and farther from the head, and the perimeter of our nighttime encampments also extended well beyond the circle of Yosef's household. We became a village on the move, and local farmers and other vendors visited our camp with their oxcarts to hawk their wares: freshly baked bread, fruits and vegetables, legs of lamb, wineskins of new wine, or barley beer poured from large vases.

Each day's journey ended by mid-afternoon, well before the sun dipped in the west, to allow time to set up tents, tend to livestock, and prepare suppers. I was usually the last to arrive at the table of Yosef and the elaborate fare, under the circumstances, prepared by his servants under the supervision of Hannah, his wife. Rahab eagerly joined in as one the servants.

The first day's journey brought the caravan to the mouth of the Yarmuk River where it emptied into the Jordan. The Yarmuk was the principal tributary into the Jordan. On the morrow, the caravan would ford the river and then turn east to follow the Yarmuk Valley toward the Hawran Plateau, which was better known by its Greco-Roman name as Auranitis.

I cautiously entered Yosef's travel tent. It was much smaller than the principal tent used during the Pella sojourn, but it still dominated the encampment. Though I knew I was expected, I nevertheless felt an interloper.

"Hello Master," Hava teased as she bustled about with her mother, finalizing supper preparations.

By overstating my title, she understated my actual importance, and I hadn't yet figured out how to respond. Though I knew I was being mocked, I was not insulted, and I didn't believe she intended any offense.

I squatted on pillows next to Yosef. A servant set a massive pot in the center, and Hava dished out steaming bowls of mutton stew, thick with carrots and peppers and flavored with leeks. I hadn't eaten all day, and I washed down three bowls of stew with barley beer and soaked up the last of the stew with chunks of bread torn from fresh loaves. When I finished, I stood up and said I would make my rounds through the encampment.

"I'll go with you," Hava said.

To walk alone with a woman seemed highly unusual, but she was the blood representative of the caravan host, after all, and who was I to object? Though she wore a scarf over her hair and around her neck, her face remained unveiled, which also seemed rather untraditional.

My rounds included greeting the hangers-on. I wanted to know who traveled with the caravan. One group, a cluster of eight or ten men, remained aloof. Without tents, they slept under the stars, near but not too near the main camp. They were an odd bunch in hair shirts, a rough weave of goat or camel hair that appeared scratchy and uncomfortable, sometimes called sackcloth and worn as a sign of mourning or penitence. Their unruly long hair had never seen a comb and their matted beards never a razor. When I greeted them, they nodded or bowed but spoke no words, and by their manner, I understood they had no interest in conversation, but it would be a long journey, and my curiosity would bring me back.

By the time the reddish sun squatted on the westerly hills, I finished my rounds, and I escorted Hava to her tent. By then, her teasing ways ceased, and she turned serious.

"Thank you," she said, "and thank you for what you do for my father. He depends upon you, and his trust is well-earned."

After the tent flap closed behind her, her perfume lingered, and I breathed deeply.

The sun peaked over the eastern ridge as the caravan stretched out the next morning. The winding Yarmuk spilled through a narrow valley with steep slopes on both sides, and the caravan snaked along the riverbanks that ascended toward the plateau. It was a slow slog, but the terrain along the lush riverbanks of the Yarmuk would be more hospitable than later. Water was plentiful for the livestock and so was the grass. I moved fore and aft on my horse splashing through the river.

"Move on. Move on. The trail widens ahead," I encouraged. "Step it up. Step it up."

Our encampment that night was adjacent to a village, and villagers supplied the wayfarers with fruits and vegetables, still-warm bread, and freshly-butchered meat for those that could pay. Hannah's table featured vegetables fried in olive oil with cantaloupe and yogurt to finish. Once again, Hava accompanied me on my rounds.

For three days, the caravan slowly climbed toward the high plains east of the Sea of Galilee. When we came to a fork in the river, we followed to the left and headed north. On the fourth day, the single-file caravan spread out as the narrow valley opened into grasslands, fields, and gentle hills of the Yarmuk plains.

"We shall pause here an extra day and allow the herds to rest and fill their bellies before we turn north, and the lands become arid," I announced to the heads of families.

After supper that evening, I wanted to engage the men in sackcloth.

"Perhaps they are intimidated by a woman in their presence," I said to Hava. "Allow me to speak to them alone."

When she started to protest, her father touched his lips with a finger, and she sighed.

"All right," she said, "but tomorrow we ride together to scout the plains."

I walked just outside the main encampment and sat down at the campfire of the men in sackcloth. I held up a plump wineskin and looked into the eyes of each in turn, but they all shook their head and didn't accept my offer.

"Then I'll drink alone," I said, and I squeezed out a full measure of red wine into my clay cup.

"What city do you call home?" I asked.

For a few moments, all were silent, but then a spokesman stepped out of the shadows. Tall and gaunt, he appeared older than the others with sparse hair on his head and a gnarled white beard that stretched nearly to his belly.

"We're not city dwellers," he said.

"Where are you going?" I asked.

"Only the Lord knows."

"Why do you journey?" I asked.

"Why do you journey?" The elder responded with the same question and a look that said, *Are you a fool? We flee the Romans like the rest.*

"Will you drink with me?" I asked.

"We don't mean to be ungrateful for your friendliness," the elder replied, "but strong drink does not touch our lips; we will be happy to share sweet dates with you."

A man appeared with a sack of dates that were passed around. I set my wineskin on the ground and accepted a handful of fruit. The group seemed friendlier than on my first visit.

"We have heard you and Yosef's clan and many in this caravan are followers of Yeshua," the elder's statement sounded like a question.

I nodded. "It's true."

"I knew him. He was one of us."

I choked on a date. Someone handed me a water skin, and I sipped several swallows.

With each word out of the old man's mouth, I grew more curious. Who was this elder who claims Yeshua was one of them? Who were these men and their scratchy shirts of camel hair?

"I was there the day Yeshua was baptized in the river," the old man continued. "He was one of many who came in those days."

I knew well the tradition that Yeshua had been baptized in the Jordan.

"By Yochanan the baptizer?" I asked. Even now, nearly four decades later, the figure of Yochanan loomed large. He raised quite a stir in his day.

Now it was the old man's turn to be surprised.

"You know his name?" the elder asked. "We are disciples of Yochanan."

For the first time, his expression changed. The slight upturn at the corners of his mouth said he was pleased. He squatted down next to me.

"Yochanan spoke to a deep yearning in the Judeans and Galileans who had grown disaffected with the corrupt temple priesthood. He offered a nearness to God that temple sacrifice did not. Even Pharisees and Sadducees heeded the call to come and change and be changed. Of course, when you challenge authority ..."

His voice trailed off, and I assumed our conversation was over, but as I stood up and turned to leave, he spoke again.

"'In the wilderness prepare the way of Yahweh, make straight in the desert a highway for our God,'" the elder recited the words slowly while nodding his head. "We heed the call of Esaias the prophet."

I smiled inwardly. This band of ascetics in sackcloth and unkempt hair looked like prophets of old. Indeed, there were some who said that Yochanan was the return of the prophet Elijah. Yet, there was something troubling about these followers of Yochanan the baptizer, and it wasn't merely their appearance. A comment of the elder echoed in my thoughts.

171

"Yeshua learned his message as a disciple of Yochanan," the elder had said.

I picked up a stick and poked in the coals. Yeshua a disciple of Yochanan?

Who was the greater and who was the lesser?

Chapter Twenty-three

"Catch me if you can," Hava said, and her bay mare broke into a gallop.

I lost sight of Hava over a hilltop, and when I finally caught up, she was on foot, delighting in crimson tulips. The horses munched on grass while we fumbled with small talk. We spoke of flowers and bird's nests and field mice. We discussed the weather and the seasons. When Hava spoke of her childhood in Arimathea, we made progress. More still when I described Damascus and what Hava could expect in the ancient city of the Aramaeans, the ancestors of the Jews. We wondered at the death of our friend, Anina, but we couldn't make sense of it. Hava confided in her worry over her former husband who ran off to Jerusalem although she acknowledged that she hadn't yet learned to love him in their arranged marriage. I peeled away layers of the emotional bandages that had covered the hole in my heart at the deaths of those closest to me, and I was surprised to sense that the wound was healing, at least it seemed so on days such as this and in present company.

After a while, we sat on a promontory overlooking the expansive Yarmuk plain. A gentle breeze rippled through the grasses creating waves. There was a timeless rhythm to the pastoral plain, an ebb and flow that made sense.

"The land is so peaceful," she said, "but humans are not."

Long, silent moments passed as we basked in the serenity.

Late in the morning before the sun had reached its peak, we mounted our horses and headed toward a nearby village. We allowed our horses a slow pace, not too anxious for the end of an idyllic morning.

We found what we were looking for in the village. A pudding vendor stirred an aromatic stew bubbling in a cast iron cauldron that dangled over an open fire. Fresh air and a hearty appetite made for a delicious stew.

"What are these bony chunks of meat?" Hava asked as she finished her bowl.

"Ham hocks," the vendor said. "Would you like another bowl?"

Hava lifted her eyebrows as her eyes peered at me with a devilish sparkle. I shrugged.

"Yes, please. Fill it up," she said and extended her bowl toward the vendor.

We each downed several bowls of ham hock stew while listening to the chatty vendor tell stories of his village. Just as we were about to leave, I felt a tug at the back of my robe, and I turned to find a young girl, perhaps four or five years old, pleading with her eyes. She wore only a tattered and grungy tunic, her hair was matted, and her fingers were grubby. She opened her mouth, but only an unintelligible raspy squeak came out. As I handed my empty bowl to the vendor, the youngster released my robe and followed the bowl.

"Apologies, sir," the vendor said. "This waif showed up a few days ago, and we don't know what to do with her. Prob'ly abandoned by country folks. Near as we can tell, she's a deaf mute, and I made the mistake of giving her a bowl of stew, and now we can't get rid of her."

Hava crouched down, took the girl's hands in her own, looked into her eyes, and spoke slowly. "Do you have a name?" A wide-eyed stare was the only response. Releasing one hand but holding the other, Hava stood up to face the vendor. "Give her a bowl of stew. I'll pay for it."

"If the lady wishes, but it's a mistake."

174

The sun had crossed over and begun its descent toward the west when we began our ride back to the caravan. Once again, we rode silently, but the blissful aura of the morning had given way to soul-searching. At least, that's what I read in the tight lips, wrinkled forehead, and drawn cheeks of my companion. Her dimples had disappeared, her nut-brown skin had blanched, and the sparkle in her eyes darkened. After riding a short distance, her horse broke into a canter, and I followed. When our encampment came into view, her bay mare released into a full gallop, and I lagged.

By the time I entered the tent of Yosef, father and daughter already argued.

"Prayer, you say? It's not your problem, you say? God will provide, you say?"

This was a side of Hava I had not seen. Angry. Confrontational. Argumentative.

"We shall not fill our bellies while the child starves," she said, and with her arm, she raked the dishware from the squat-legged table and sent plates and bowls clattering into a heap of broken shards.

"Why is it when men seek to be instruments of God's will, it means taking up sword and spear? Or, endless waiting, waiting, waiting for God to intervene? The time is not right, but soon the reign will come, the wise men say. Well, I say God will not intervene in the silly wars of men nor save Jerusalem from her folly. God's reign is not in some fanciful future but here and now. God's reign will not arrive in the clouds over Jerusalem but is already present in that village on the hillside where a child awaits the helping hands of God. And here they are!"

175

With that, Hava waved her open palms in her father's face, wheeled, and stomped out of the tent. Over her shoulder, she proclaimed, "I will not allow that child to perish for want of love, much less food."

Within seconds, her bay mare whinnied, and the sounds of galloping hooves were swallowed up by the din of the camp.

I felt embarrassed for my patron, but the squat aristocrat from Arimathea did not appear fazed. With a shrug, he said, "'Twill take a strong man to be husband to that one." He dismissed me with a wave and a command. "Follow her. Make sure she and the child have a safe return from the village. Already the sun sinks low."

The sun had set, and a large bonfire encircled by Yosef's tents provided the only light when we returned with the child. Yosef and Hannah, his wife, emerged from their tent and a few servant faces peeked through the flap of another tent. The wide eyes of the child were filled with confusion and apprehension. Rahab stepped forward into the aura of the fire.

"With your permission, I shall mind the child," she said.

Rahab knelt on one knee with arms extended. The child hesitated, then took a cautious step forward.

"Come, come, dear one," Rahab said, and the tips of her fingers beckoned the child.

Suddenly, the child rushed forward into Rahab's arms. Rahab clutched her close as tears streamed down her face.

"You will be loved," Rahab said, squeezing the child tight.

Hava moved forward, squatted, and draped one arm over the shoulder of Rahab and one over the shoulder of the deaf-mute child.

"Ahuva," Hava said.

She repeated the name again, slowly, with exaggerated movement of her lips as her face came up close against the child's."

"'Ahuva' shall be your name, for you shall be beloved."

Chapter Twenty-four

After a day of rest, the caravan departed refreshed and early. Our number grew by one deaf-mute child. The trail was broader, flatter, and quicker now that we reached the high ground. We followed a narrow corridor of passable terrain north through the oak forests of the plateau known as the lava lands. To our left lay the rugged hills and gullies of Bashan with rivers and their valleys falling away to the west; to the east, the Syrian Desert loomed.

By midday, the snow-capped triple peaks of Mt. Hermon came into view. The white-haired eminences that presided over the valley and Damascus had been with me all the days of my youth. Perhaps Mother cast her eyes on the mount at this very moment, and I felt very close yet very far. With the sighting of the familiar mountain, it seemed the pace of the caravan crawled more slowly than ever.

The caravan trail meandered through fields of grain and past small villages. Barley was always the first to be harvested, and the threshers were busy in the fields; barley shocks that appeared as shaggy beasts lurked in the stubble. The first fruits became locally brewed beer, and local farmers gladly sold it to the caravans from tall vases out of the back of their wagons.

Though the region was farmland with plenty of rain in season, there were no lakes or streams and only a few springs in the basalt rock of ages-old lava flow. Over the centuries, the caravans learned the locations of the springs, and they became familiar waypoints on the caravan trails. With each morning's departure, I had another watering hole in mind as our afternoon destination, but this day there would be a problem. My high spirits quickly dissipated when the watering hole came into view. Smoke from multiple campfires appeared as a slab of slate hanging over the greenery of the oasis. Gray tent tops peeked through low-lying bushes. A dozen horses were hobbled and staked in a grassy patch. According to local knowledge, there would not be another watering hole for a full day's journey, but this one was occupied.

I stopped the caravan on a promontory overlooking the olive grove that marked the watering hole. While Yosef and I considered our options, a trio of riders kicked up dust in a hasty approach from the grove. My breathing quickened as three Roman officers reined up next to us.

"Are you the leaders of this caravan?" asked their officer.

I nodded.

"Our centurion invites you to water your livestock and fill your water skins. Tis a small woodland, and there is not space for your camp, but you may pitch your tents here and come and go to the springs for water as you need."

The shifty eyes of the legionaries didn't inspire confidence. Yosef's knit eyebrows and pinched cheeks said what I already knew; we had no other options, and we must trust the hospitality of the Romans.

Servants led the livestock in small herds back and forth to the watering hole; except for the camels, the animals would perish without water at least once a day. I set double watches throughout the night although Yosef's entourage would be helpless under a full-scale raid by the Romans, and the guards would only be effective against the odd, larcenous soldier. The camp followers rested in place without setting up tents. If the Romans raided the main camp, the hangers-on would slip away.

Through the night, I wandered about the camp but always with quick glances in the direction of the oasis that seemed peaceful enough under a

179

sliver of a waning moon. Keen ears captured every rustling mouse in the grass and the beating wings of the bats that flitted about. When a horse whinnied, I hoped it was merely a passing fox or striped hyena and not creeping Romans. If the Romans came, we were all doomed, and I knew it; as the moon set and the night darkened, my anxiety deepened, but the night passed without incident.

With the first glow over the eastern desert, I roused the caravan for an early departure. As we passed by the Roman encampment, servants peeled off and delivered a fine young colt as tribute for the centurion.

We reached the next watering hole as planned. After a supper of bread and chickpea stew, I made my customary rounds, and I returned to the campfire circle of the reclusive group dressed in sackcloth; I returned their earlier hospitality with my own bag of dates.

Once again, the gaunt elder was the spokesman for the disciples of Yochanan the baptizer, and he seemed downright chatty compared to earlier discussions.

"Tell me more about Yochanan. Tell me more about the day that Yeshua was baptized," I asked, and then I listened while the elder jabbered.

"For many who came to change and be changed in the waters of the River Jordan, baptism was a powerful, moving, spiritual experience. So, it was for Yeshua. When he rose up from the waters, he sobbed before he cast his eyes toward the heavens with arms outstretched. When he returned to the riverbank, his face glowed. I know that God touched his heart that day, and he heard God call his name."

The old man breathed deeply, and his whole body rocked forward and back on his walking stick as he remembered. Once again, I thought our conversation was over, but when I prepared to leave, the elder spoke again.

"Yochanan spoke the truth at the cost of his life. When he criticized the evil marriage of the king, he was imprisoned and eventually executed. Such is the way of the world." His rocking back and forth quickened. "Such is the way of the world. Such is the way of the world." Suddenly, the rocking stopped, and he cast his eyes toward the heavens. "We must all speak the truth and accept the consequences," his voice lowered to a whisper, "even at the risk of death."

After a long pause, he drew a deep breath and turned his face toward me. "Your leader understood. When Yochanan was imprisoned, Yeshua returned to the Galilee, and he spoke truth to authority even though he understood the possible consequences." The rocking began again.

As I exited the aura of the campfire, the elder mumbled after me. "Speak the truth, lad. Speak the truth, whatever the cost."

The next morning, the brilliant crimson sunrise troubled me. The whole eastern sky glowed as the pomegranate sun peeked over the horizon. I wiped a finger around the rim of my clay cup, and I grimaced--dust not dew. Damascus was close, and our journey's end was only a couple of days away, but now our trail would pass through harsh lands, and a desert storm threatened. We had come under the lee of the range of Mt. Hermon, and the mountains were a rain catcher, draining the sea winds of their moisture: the westward slopes were moist and verdant, but the plateau to the east of the mountains was dry and arid.

At midday, the sun stood still. It was the solstice, the longest day of the year, and it would seem endless. Our caravan was a league down the

181

road when the wind picked up. Mount Hermon disappeared, and the sun became a faint orange ball. An east wind, a *ruach qadim*, lifted sand and dust from the desert just a short distance to the east. By mid-afternoon, the intensity of the windstorm forced the caravan to stop. The servants at the head awaited my instructions. They had lost the trail.

Yosef and I huddled together behind our horses to shield us from the wind and sand. The prominent eyebrows of the old man were caked in dust.

"Shall we cluster here and wait till the storm blows itself out?" I asked with the hint of a suggestion.

Yosef patted the neck of his horse. The goats and cattle and horses already appeared stressed.

"Who can know the wind?" Yosef said. "Will it be an hour or a day?"

It could be more. I knew these desert storms. Animals would soon begin to perish without water, but …

"If we move, we will wander aimlessly. We may end up in the desert or at the edge of a cliff," I said.

To me, it seemed prudent to wait. The easy solution was to do nothing.

"Look back at the caravan." Yosef said. "What do you see?"

I couldn't see much. Bundled in robes and headdresses, Hava and Hannah were mere clumps atop camels led by servants; the string of pack donkeys that followed faded into the dust. What did Yosef want me to see?

"It's a line. Don't you see? It's a straight line. It's like an arrow pointing the way forward."

I was skeptical, and I reluctantly urged the caravan onward. I looked forward, then back, then forward again. I felt my way with my own feet, glancing back every few steps to keep my path straight. When I moved, one hand extended in front as if I could feel the way even if I couldn't see. The others followed, grasping the robe of the one in front or the tail of a donkey. I had become Bartimaeus the blind beggar with a trail of trusting followers tightly clutching a rope line, but who led me? To lose our way was unthinkable, but how could I not think of it? Dangerous gullies were near to our left and a lifeless desert to our right.

I was fearful of the dangers on all sides, but mostly I felt the pain of inadequacy. I was a simple scribe, a natural born follower not a leader.

The sand-stinging gales stirred memories of the vortex that sucked away all that I held dear, all that I was, all that I hoped to be. Had the tempest merely circled around the mountains and around the years, lurking in the desert, stalking me, awaiting my return to swallow up the rest? Our caravan toiled under the sun to get this far, propelled forward by the hope of Eden, but was our journey merely vanity? What is crooked cannot be made straight, and I was terrified that we were merely chasing after wind.

Yet, I continued to place one foot in front of the other.

I pictured myself a child at play with Rufus and Alexander, splashing and laughing in the Barada River. Mother sat in the shade on the shore, and Papa was there as well; it was rare that my long-dead father would appear in my consciousness, but there he was, plucking ripe apricots from the branches, sucking the sweet pulp while juices dribbled into his black beard, and then tossing the pits into the river ... splash, splash, splash. The circle of ripples spread wider and wider and wider.

I paused to wipe sand out of my eyes and reset my wrapped headdress. I looked back at the caravan line, but I could only see Yosef, his wife, and his daughter on their camels; if the others followed, I

183

couldn't tell. Once again, I willed each step forward, one foot in front of the other, arm extended, pointing the way.

My memories moved forward to my wedding day, and the young bride who allowed me to love her, and then forward again to Rehum who sacrificed his life for my own. I splashed about in the pool with blind Bartimaeus, and I wrestled again with the strange river beast on the banks of the Jordan who strangely called me the virile one who would be the father of many. Then the face of Anina smiled at me, filled with hope. My life held meaning, she said. My life held purpose, she said. I so wanted to believe her, to trust her, even amid this maelstrom, as I took each halting step forward.

Suddenly, a guttural bellow pierced the wind, like the cry of a bleating goat only deeper and louder. I stopped in my tracks as Hava's camel trotted past me. I lunged forward to follow the beast as it disappeared into a maze of tall, spindly shapes; at first, I imagined long men, giants really, and I feared we had bumped into a phalanx of Roman legionaries with lances held high and ready to strike. But the shapes were not human; they were tree trunks in the swirling dust. My extended hand scraped against the rough bark of a palm tree, and I stopped in place. I wiped my eyes, and a whole grove shimmered before me. Hava's camel had smelled spring water. I dropped to my knees, and my whole body convulsed in sobs. Thanks be to God!

In the cover of the oasis, the wind and the dust seemed less, and we set up tents, and the animals drank deeply of sweet water, and campfires were lit, and babies cried, and children laughed, and we survived the dust storm of the *ruach qadim*. Thanks be to God!

Many stopped by and slapped me on the back or shouted, "well done", but I knew better. I had been as lost as the rest of them and stumbling upon the oasis was pure miracle. Thanks be to God!

Hava stood behind me and smiled at the well-wishers.

"Sit," she said after the last one departed.

I did as she commanded, and she rubbed a balm of aloe on my wind-burned face. Whether it was the balm or the touch of her hand, the sting of the sand was healed in an instant. It also occurred to me that my knee was free of pain, and my steps through the desert winds had been pure without a limp.

The wind howled through the night and all the next day, and our caravan remained in place in the shelter of the palms. And then, suddenly, dead calm. The storm ended. The dust still lingered high in the sky, and the late afternoon sun hovering over the mountains to the west was crimson but cool. The crisis ceased and, normalcy returned. That night, a few villagers appeared with an ox cart of tall jugs filled with barley malt, and they sold every drop.

I rose early the next morning; in the first twinkling of dawn, I saw the haze, the smoke from many hearths hanging over Damascus in a flat, blue sheet. Hava appeared at my side and grasped my arm, and together we watched the sunrise.

With great energy and excitement, the caravan departed for the last leg of our journey. For days, we had been trudging toward Mt. Hermon, but now the range of mountains moved to our left side. We crossed highways and trails, spokes of a wheel extending from the Damascus hub. We encountered foot traffic, horsemen, ox carts, and itinerant merchants leading sway-backed donkeys. By mid-afternoon, we reached the banks of the Barada, the golden stream that rushed out of the mountains and spilled into the great oasis known as the Ghouta. For longer than men could remember, this oasis had been sanctuary, settlement, and site of Damascus, and once the land of Jacob before his tribe moved on to the land God promised.

Yosef's entourage pitched tents and set up camp on the banks of the Barada, outside the city walls. The camp followers departed, no longer in need of the protections of a caravan. I resisted the urge to ride into the city immediately. I knew of a private cove, and there we bathed, washing away the impurities of our journey, a rite of initiation into a new life and a new community.

Mount Hermon 69-70 CE

Then Moses went up on the mountain, and the cloud covered the mountain. The glory of the LORD settled on Mount Sinai, and the cloud covered it for six days; on the seventh day he called to Moses out of the cloud. As he came down from the mountain with the two tablets of the covenant in his hand, Moses did not know that the skin of his face shone because he had been talking with God.

Exodus 24:15-16 & 34:29

Chapter Twenty-five

Her beauty endured. Reddish-orange hair had ripened into a rich auburn, her ruddy face beamed, and her sage-green eyes sparkled. The slender woman remained vibrant nearing her sixtieth birthday.

When I returned to my childhood home, I stood momentarily in the doorway and watched Charis, my mother, stirring a bubbling stew over the hearth. Her wooden spoon landed on the dirt floor when she spied me. She scooped up her house dress and rushed to me, clutching me close and stroking my hair, but quickly she held me at arm's length to soak in my face. There was laughter in her eyes-the joy of a mother embracing her child--but sadness also. The world had turned since we were last together. If she hadn't aged, I had. She held my robe open and shook her head at the bony frame under my tunic. Quickly, she added a bowl and spoon to the table and set out flat loaves and yogurt, and I ate heartily.

I remembered my father returning to this same room, sitting at the same table after his day's work. What I remembered most was bouncing on Abba's knee. He smiled broadly and teased while I giggled. But then Abba took ill and died suddenly, leaving his wife a widow and his child fatherless. Sometimes I blamed God; other times I was angry with my absent father; but mostly, I blamed myself for no good reason. There was no sense to it, but that didn't lessen the tinge of guilt on the edge of grief. On the journey from Pella, as my anticipation of homecoming swelled, I sometimes imagined that my father would be there.

I slept soundly in my familiar bed and awoke early. Before seeking my friends, Rufus and Alexander, I navigated the familiar haunts of the city of my youth. My nose remembered the scents of Damascus: aromatic jasmine from the shrubs and vines of the Ghouta, sausages sizzling on vendors' grills in the market, and fresh-baked loaves on many hearths. The old city weathered the centuries well; as a major terminus on the caravan routes connecting east and west, Damascus enjoyed a healthy commerce. But it was a city on the edge as well. East grated against west, and Damascus squatted atop the fault line between the Arabic reign of Nabataea and the Roman Empire. In the absence of strong authority, petty thieves and prostitutes flourished. My mother was the daughter of an anonymous Roman soldier and an Aramaic prostitute who abandoned her daughter at a young age, a trifling thing to my mother that only confirmed that she was a child of God. But, knowing that my grandparents were a prostitute and a Roman soldier had always been a prickly irritant to me.

Under watchful eyes, I followed a circular route through the winding, narrow streets and alleyways of the city, skirting the Nabatean sector, passing through the Greco-Roman precincts, before I returned to the Jewish neighborhood that included the Iesou community. The old city walls had not prevented the animosity in Judea and the Galilee from seeping into Damascus. There was tension in the city that was new since I had departed a few years earlier, and invisible walls had risen to separate the sectors. The Jews had been bullied and became an insular community within their own neighborhoods: the followers of Iesou a smaller cloister yet, shunned, or worse, by Jew and Gentile alike. As I brazenly toured the city streets, suspicion followed me.

I passed by the building that backed against the city wall that had been the scene of the famous escape of Paulos the apostle in a basket lowered from the ramparts. Paulos was a revered figure in the local Iesou community. He spent three years of his early career in Damascus, and my mother and father had been close intimates of the man from Tarsos, but I

189

was too young to have personal memories. Even after Paulos left Damascus, he resided for more than a decade in nearby Antioch as a leader of the growing Iesou community of that city. If the Yeshua community of Pella was under the sphere of influence of Jewish Jerusalem, Damascus looked north to Antioch and the Gentile branch of the Iesou community. Even the respective names, Yeshua in Hebrew/Aramaic and Iesou in Greek, reflected differences between the communities.

After my memory-jogging tour of the city, I arrived at the warehouse of Rufus and Alexander. The brothers were brokers, handling goods and transshipments here at the intersection of east and west, where the camel caravans of the orient first encountered the wealthy consumers of the Roman Empire. The first thing I noticed was that the warehouse was mostly empty, and there was little activity.

Rufus was there alone, and we shared a warm embrace. He was thinner and so was his hair. A lot had changed in two years. He greeted me with a wan smile, and he scooped a cup of red wine from a tall jar for me before refilling his own cup.

"Business is bad," he said as I scanned the empty warehouse. "No caravans with the war nearby. Some slide south for the port in Gaza, but most pass to the north: Antioch or up the Tigris River along the Old Persian Royal Road."

"Let me fill up your cup." I had barely touched my wine, but Rufus drained his own cup and refilled it. "Let the Romans finish their business and then maybe the caravans will return."

That the Romans would conquer Jerusalem was a foregone conclusion among all segments of the Damascus population, and I couldn't disagree.

My next stop was our local synagogue, the one that remained a sanctuary to the followers of Iesou. My mother's blood had been spilled on the synagogue steps. As a youngster, I heard the story often. Paulos the apostle had first persecuted the local followers of Iesou before his miraculous transformation on the road to Damascus. My mother had been whipped right here at the synagogue entrance by the man who would later become her dear friend, and the pale scars on her arms served as reminders. Later, she befriended him and nourished him with wine, bread, and a word of forgiveness in a storm-tossed forest glen on a mountain road near Damascus. The next morning, she witnessed his baptism in a mountain stream. After that, Paulos became an important member of the Damascus congregation until he barely escaped the authorities three years later. "Paulos the provocateur" his mother called him and always with a smile. After his escape, Paulos settled in Antioch and letters and visitors often passed between the two communities.

I stepped between marble pillars into the main room of the synagogue. The Hellenistic Jews of this house of prayer had long been followers of Iesou who adapted their Hebrew rituals to celebrate the life, death, and resurrection of the christos, but much of the congregation was Gentile. After hesitating briefly in the main hall, I stepped quickly into an anteroom. The small room was lined with cabinets that bulged with papyrus scrolls. I ran my fingers along the shelf marked "The Prophets". Other shelves were marked "Torah" and "The Writings".

In my youth, these old scrolls held no meaning, but I now felt compelled to read and search for answers to questions that had bubbled up during my experiences of the last few years.

191

Following a restless night, I awoke shivering. After I rekindled a fire in the hearth from the embers of the night before, I gnawed on stale bread as I stepped into the courtyard behind the house. Winter sometimes visited Damascus, and a veneer of snow covered the ground, but the morning sky dawned clear. Mt. Hermon and the mountain range appeared especially close this morning with fingers of snow extending down the ridges toward the city. Heavy, icy breaths clouded around my face as I chipped through thin ice in the water vase to fill a pair of pitchers. I sniffed the gathering breeze that blew chilly from the west. Mother was baking fresh bread, but I couldn't wait. I chomped down a few slices of cold lamb, and then I was off to Yosef's encampment outside the city walls. The west wind whistled through the Damascus streets, biting my face.

Yosef had not yet been able to purchase a suitable villa in Damascus. Though he had plenty of gold, silver, and livestock, neither Gentile nor Jew would entertain any purchase offers from the expatriate who fled his homeland and who claimed allegiance neither to Rome nor to Jerusalem but to a long-dead mashiah. Relations between the Damascus factions were combustible enough without splashing oil in the flames that licked at the city's calm. I carried news of the latest rejection to Yosef as I passed through the city gates.

I didn't know it then, but I was about to meet the King of the Jews.

A few days earlier, on the far slopes of the mountain range, a royal entourage departed the city of Caesarea Philippi for the fifty-mile journey to Damascus. The great-grandson of King Herod the Great, Marcus Julius Agrippa, was reared in Rome as a prince in the Imperial Court, and Emperor Claudius later appointed the noble to be King of the Jews and dispatched him to Palestine. After Claudius' assassination, King Herod

Agrippa II deftly switched his allegiance to the boy-emperor Nero by renaming Caesarea Philippi, the city to the north of the Galilee, "Neronias" in honor of the young monarch. When the conflagration in Jerusalem began and the rebels from the Galilee threatened not just the Romans but the Hebrew royalty and aristocracy, King Herod Agrippa II fled to Neronias, which would become his stronghold during the civil war that raged to the south. After Nero's suicide, the city name reverted to Caesarea Philippi. When the armies of General Vespasian passed through the city enroute to make war on the rebels, the King of the Jews hosted the General's staff and sent two thousand archers to support the Roman siege of Jerusalem. Jews loyal to the king would kill the Jewish rebels.

This, then, was the nature of the royalty that circled around the base of Mt. Hermon enroute to Damascus. Favorable tides of war lifted the king and carried him forward. The prince from the imperial Roman court sided with the soon-to-be victors, and now he intended to claim his booty.

Along with other foot travelers on the road from Damascus, I was shunted to the side by the phalanx of royal bodyguards.

"Make way for the king. Make way for the king."

Agrippa didn't sit his horse well. The corpulent, red-robed sovereign appeared as a blob of butter oozing over a strawberry tart. Heedless of the others he passed by, the king's slit-eyes set over puffy cheeks fastened upon me, the lowly scribe from Damascus.

My curiosity instantly turned to foreboding when the entourage turned off the main road onto a side trail, the pathway to Yosef's encampment. I left my place at the side of the road and sprinted ahead with the bitter west wind chasing from behind; each footfall increased my dread as I neared Yosef's tents. I arrived just moments ahead of the king's vanguard. Yosef emerged from his tent with a puzzled expression as I breathlessly blurted that royal visitors would soon arrive. Yosef always wore a tall turban except when reclining on soft pillows in his tent, but now I looked down upon his bare, bald head. The man seemed so short, and his stooped shoulders only made him the smaller. Yosef looked at me, then at the troops entering his encampment, then he looked over his shoulder at his unprepared servants and family. The overnight snowfall melted in the noonday sun, leaving the yard a muddy mess. Hava and her mother, Hannah, stood at the edge of their tent's entrance, with the loose canvas fly flapping in the breeze. Peeking from another tent, Ahuva, the deaf-mute child, clutched Rahab's robes.

The king's soldiers formed a double line facing inward, and the king's prancing stallion passed between the rows. The king jerked on the reins as he arrived at the place where Yosef and I waited. We bowed awkwardly.

"Are you the traitor from Arimathea?" the king asked in a squeaky voice.

Yosef was nonplussed. "No, no, I am not a traitor, Sire, but, but yes I do hail from Arimathea. You see, you see, I have moved my household away from the dangerous brigands from the Galilee."

The king's jowls waggled as he chewed on the aristocrat's answer, and then he scanned the encampment.

Yosef gestured toward a stew pot hanging over hot coals. "I offer the king a meager meal. Had we known you were coming, we would have butchered a calf and prepared a feast."

The king ignored the invitation, and his gaze fixed on the herds that grazed nearby. He gently nudged his stallion forward with a slight kick to its ribs, and the king and several mounted bodyguards rode amongst the cattle, goats, horses, and camels that comprised Yosef's fortune. As we watched helplessly, the king's men began to gather Yosef's herds.

Born into a prosperous family, Yosef knew himself only as a wealthy man, and now his mean status fit poorly, and tears streamed down his wrinkled cheeks as the king stole his wealth and perhaps his identity. But there would be more.

As the livestock slopped their way down the muddy pathway, shepherded by the king's men, the King returned to us. By then, Hava and her mother joined us, each clutching Yosef's forearms. Yosef seemed a phantom in a stranger's pelt, and his pallid skin draped loosely over a hollowed frame. So, too, his wife who cowered under the king's glare, but daughter Hava's eyes bulged with rage.

"I am sure you are only too happy to contribute toward the war effort against those brigands who frighten you so," the king mocked. "Is there more you would volunteer? Perhaps there is gold and silver stored in chests in your tents?"

The king waved at waiting soldiers who methodically ransacked the tents. They stole jewelry and chests of gold coins. Ill-tempered Agrippa rhythmically tapped his crop against his leg, and then, with a final, loud whack on his stallion's hind quarter, the horse lurched forward, and we fell back in unison. The king leaned in close and stretched his crop to stroke Hava's chin.

"I claim this one also. I am sure she will serve well as a servant in my private chambers."

Hannah fainted, Hava and Yosef slapped and pushed and kicked against the guards who grabbed her, and I lunged for her, but I was

195

wrestled to the ground by bodyguards who pointed their swords at my neck as I lay helpless in the mud. I couldn't see her struggles, but I heard Hava's insults as the guards led her away, and the screams of the child filled the camp.

Chapter Twenty-six

"Fetch Rufus and Alexander," I said. "Tell them to bring swords and four horses." A pair of Yosef's servants hurried off to Damascus.

Yosef was torn between good sense and hope. He half-heartedly attempted to talk me out of pursuing the King's soldiers, yet he yearned for a miracle despite the improbability of rescue of his child.

My loyal friends appeared in Yosef's plundered camp by nightfall, and we set out down the road after dark. For the despondent brothers who had languished in the chaos and ill will of Damascus, this quest rekindled a fire in their bellies that I had not seen since we escaped Jerusalem.

"Whatever happens," I counseled Yosef, "there will be reprisals, and you and yours should seek safe sanctuary." Neither of us knew where that might be.

The encampment of the king was not far down the road, and we sidled off into side brush when camp fires appeared. Rufus remained with the horses while Alexander and I crept closer, crabbing forward on elbows and knees. The night watch was sparse as the king and his lieutenants didn't expect any audacious visitors. A pair of sentinels leaned on lances in front of the largest tent; undoubtedly, the king slept inside. We couldn't know if Hava was there also. A few soldiers tended the fires. Only one other tent had a guard posted, and he appeared to be asleep on his haunches, leaning against his *cuirass* that had been removed from his torso; the point of his lance stuck into the sand, and his *galeas* perched on top with the feathered plume softly flickering in the night breeze. We trusted our luck and hoped that was the tent where she slept.

My *gladius* remained sheathed on my hip as I instinctively reached for my *pugio*. When I first tasted battle, racing down the slopes of Beth

Horon, shouting war whoops and stabbing at the air with my feeble hunting knife, I was a foolish innocent. Now, I was a calculating killer. A broad, leafy bush, a Jericho Balsam, crowded against the tent on the far side, and I would make my way around and behind the tent to reach the bush. From there, I would launch my attack.

I spit in a handful of dust and rubbed my face with my palms before I began to crawl around the back of the tent. I have never been so alert, before or since. With eyes wide and black as I snaked along on my belly, the scritch-scratch of creatures scurrying away filled my ears. My lungs sucked in wood smoke from juniper branches burning in the camp fires, tickling my nostrils. When I reached the balsam clump, I paused briefly. A lark trilled in the branches to announce to all who cared that dawn was near. The guard peacefully snored in grunts and whistles as he dreamed his last dream.

When I pounced, my left fist rammed into the man's mouth and grabbed his tongue to stifle a cry as my *pugio* plunged deep between his shoulders, and I twisted the dagger to find his heart. I held him in repose for a moment, then released him into blood and sand. When I first killed, I vomited all over myself, but now I was ice, and I didn't worry about the injustice of the killing. In the defense of that which is dear, there is no morality save love, there is no essence save survival.

Alexander released from his station and rushed past me into the tent, and I followed him inside. She was there, lashed to a tent pole. After Alexander cut the cords, she nearly knocked me over as she flung her arms around me and kissed me hard on my lips, which I was not prepared for, and my warrior's concentration was broken, but Alexander retained his good sense. Without speaking, he tugged on my tunic, and we exited the tent, but we had been discovered.

There would be no slinking away into the dark, and we sprinted toward Rufus and the waiting horses. Shouts chased our heels. Hava flew onto the back of her horse, and I clumsily mounted my own as cursing soldiers arrived. I kicked my mare in the ribs, and we were off.

I wasn't aware when it happened, but as we galloped toward the golden glow of Mt. Hermon with the rising sun tickling her snowy peaks, I realized that my tunic was sticky with blood. By the time our horses slowed to a canter, a dull ache in my shoulder told me that the blood was my own and not that of the dead sentry. I said nothing as we rode higher and higher up the mountain path. By the time the slope turned slick from fresh snow, and our horses slowed to a walk, my arm and hand had turned numb, and I grasped the reins with my off hand. Still we climbed, and the steamy breath of the horses said we entered winter.

And then we raced. "Catch me if you can," she said, and I chased after her, but she soon disappeared over a rise in the undulating grasses. When I caught up to her, she was picking long, drooping, white flowers. As I dismounted, she came forward and tickled my face with the blossoms, but then she was gone, and the entire field was covered in white flowers that grew taller and taller as I watched, and they were cold, and they were icicles.

I choked on wood smoke, and my eyes watered in the stinging fumes from the fire that smoldered next to me. FIRE! I tried to sit up, but pain seared through my shoulder, and a gentle touch pushed me down again.

Shapes, shapes like humans, hovered over me. The phantom shapes were men, old men with white beards and thick, flowing white hair, and they mumbled and chanted as they floated over me. And then a younger man joined them, and his clothes beamed white, whiter than the beards of the old men, whiter than snow, whiter than bones bleached white in the sun, glowing white, radiant white, searing white, and I squeezed my eyes tight from the brightness.

My eyes blinked open, and I tried to measure my surroundings. There was a roof overhead and walls around me, but they were thin, and cold air whistled through. The hut smelled of smoke, but the embers were dying, and I shivered, and I was hungry and thirsty. When I tried to push myself up, I gasped at the pain in my shoulder, and I collapsed again onto the mat and slept.

The young man slaked my thirst with water from a skin, cool and sweet like nothing I had ever tasted. He wiped my brow, and the pounding in my head subsided. He touched my shoulder, and the pain disappeared. I tried to speak, but I could not. I tried to look into his eyes, but his robes glowed like the sun, and I could see no features. I closed my eyes. All was calm. Peacefulness settled over me and warmed me.

When I next awoke, the hut was smoky again, and someone stirred nearby. I attempted to speak, but only a raspy squeak came out. The figure turned quickly, bent over, and kissed me.

We wintered in an abandoned hunter's hut in the mountainside forest of Mt. Hermon, surviving on venison, hares, and melted snow. Rufus and Alexander did the hunting and Hava was my nurse. It was a miracle they survived, and me? Well, it was more than a miracle thanks to Hava's poultice and the visits of the heavenly figures in my dreams. Only later did I learn that Rufus had snuck into Damascus for thick, woolen cloaks with hoods, tall leather hunting boots, bows and arrows, and medicinal herbs that Hava used to prepare an olive oil unguent that she rubbed over my wound, but he also reported that he dared not stay with his wife and children because he was under suspicion, and his home was being watched. The same was true of Alexander's family. Whenever Rufus returned from his infrequent forays into Damascus, he was greeted with Hava's imploring eyes, and each time he grit his teeth and shook his head.

"No news," he said.

It seemed that Yosef, Hannah, Rahab, and the child had disappeared from the face of the earth.

As the warming spring sun melted the mountain snows, there was finally good news. The king's agents departed Damascus: Agrippa apparently forgot the four of us and focused instead on leveraging his support of Rome to his advantage.

As winter passed, so too did the soreness in my wounded shoulder, thanks to Hava's poultice. As I ventured from the hut to explore the wooded slopes, I realized that my knee pain had also departed, and I walked without a limp. I was anxious to return to Damascus, but first I must plan. Contemplating the future was a remembered pleasure. Hope had returned.

Spring breezes filtered through sighing pines as we walked on spongy ground, taking care not to step on ferns sprouting amongst the pine needles. When Hava's father had been rich, it would have been impossible for me, a lowly scribe, to approach him about a wedding contract for his

201

daughter. Now, I could not ask a man who had disappeared. And, so I did the unthinkable. I asked the daughter directly.

In the shade of the pines, we faced each other on flat rocks at the edge of a bubbling brook of melted snow from higher up the mountain. She wore a tattered goatskin robe, and her hair was matted and unkempt, and a smear of mud streaked across her cheek. I'm sure my words were clumsy, but I imagined great eloquence. In my fantasy we sat on silk pillows with Yosef to my left, Hava the daughter across, and Hannah the wife at the end of a stubby-legged table on a high-backed oak chair (the better to supervise the servants), I dressed in the best of my meager wardrobe, but the others wore flamboyant silks: maroon for Yosef, emerald green for Hava, and purple for Hannah. Brushed with the luster of olive oil, Hava's hair flowed warmly over her shoulders onto her tunic. Her emerald robe was not gathered but draped from shoulder to sandaled feet. The tunic was a lighter shade of green that was bound at the waist by a sash, highlighting her womanly curves.

Servants circled with steaming bowls of coriander and carrots, freshly baked flat bread, baked yams, and sliced avocados, centered on spicy roast lamb; yogurt and dried fruits came later. After we ate our fill, the leftovers were cleared, and Hannah left the room to supervise the servants.

After I expressed my intentions to Yosef, he replied, "Are you prepared to discuss terms? I ask no conditions but the hope that you sire many sons."

Under the swaying pines, her green eyes sparkled, and the entire forest seemed dull and gray except for splashes of vibrant shades of green that I imagined on Hava. Her emerald robe seemed alive. Her lime tunic was fresh as spring. Jade jewelry glistened. Even her pinched cheeks and

202

crimson painted lips seemed colorless next to her eyes: deep and green and wet as an oasis pool. There was no color in the world save green and no woman save Hava.

I swam in the depths of her eyes, and the imagined words of Yosef floated past like rose petals on a pond. When my wife and child died in childbirth, part of me died as well. I had been a husband, but that had died to me; I had been a lover, but that had died to me; I had been a father, but that had died to me, and the resurrection of the fullness of my being was unexpected and beyond comprehension. That I could experience such things again with Hava the angel could only be miracle. And so, I sat, dumbstruck in love floating between the fantasy and the reality.

The moment seemed eternal, but then Hava stood up from her rocky seat and moved to me, grasping my hand and tugging me to my feet. Her delicate fingers wiped my tousled hair away, and she kissed my forehead softly. I followed her gaze to the treetops and the wispy, white clouds that floated above.

"On this holy mountain, God has heard your promises," she said. "In my eyes and His, we are now wed."

She dropped her arms to my sides and grasped my tunic and lifted it high over my head. She carefully laid it atop the pine cones and needles and smoothed it out. She then removed her own tunic and laid it alongside mine and beckoned to me. I knelt before her and touched my fingers to her forehead, parting the locks that hung forward, then down along her cheeks and chin before lingering with her neck. Then, my hands glided out over her shoulders, displacing the straps of her undergarment that slipped to her waist. Our breathing quickened, and when my hands reached her breasts, a shiver rippled through her body.

"Come to me, now," she said.

How graceful are your feet in sandals, O queenly maiden!

Your rounded thighs are like jewels, the work of a master hand. Your navel is a rounded bowl that never lacks mixed wine. Your belly is a heap of wheat, encircled with lilies. Your two breasts are like two fawns, twins of a gazelle. Your neck is like an ivory tower. Your flowing locks are like purple; a king is held captive in the tresses. How fair and pleasant you are, O loved one, delectable maiden!

You are stately as a palm tree, and your breasts are like its clusters. I say I will climb the palm tree and lay hold of its branches. O may your breasts be like clusters of the vine, and the scent of your breath like apples, and your kisses like the best wine that goes down smoothly.

Damascus 70-71

My voice rings out, this time, from Damascus
It rings out from the house of my mother and father
In Sham. The geography of my body changes.
The cells of my blood become green.
My alphabet is green.
In Sham. A new mouth emerges for my mouth
A new voice emerges for my voice
And my fingers
Become a tribe.

From Damascus, What Are You Doing to Me? by Nizar Qabbani

Chapter Twenty-seven

Death drew near, and yet there was life abundant. The final assault on Jerusalem began as spring burst out all around us. As General Titus constructed massive siege towers at Jerusalem's outer walls, we meandered through mountainside fields of aromatic white jasmine. As flames licked at the temple's walls, cool spring water bubbled from under moss-covered rocks. When Jerusalem's defenses were breached, and blood-swollen gutters ran red, a rush of clear water from freshly-melted mountain snows spilled over the banks of the Barada.

In the paradox of life in the shadow of death, Hava and I discovered our Eden. I could have remained on the mountain for the remainder of my born days, but Hava had other plans.

"We must rescue the others," she said.

Her smirk teased my puzzlement, but then her face darkened.

"They wallow in despair," she said. "They are without hope. They know only oppression and the sting of death."

"True enough, but what can we do?" I asked.

"Your grip has grown accustomed to the heft of a sword and the sweep of a dagger, but these will not be your weapons," she answered. "You will use your reed pens and inks to scribe a story, to fashion a narrative from the bits and pieces that have come down to us. You will encourage and uplift our community. In a world of darkness, we have been bathed in light, and we must share that good news with the others."

I was reluctant, even obstinate, and for the next few days, I wandered alone in the forest. Then, during an evening chorus of crickets and frogs, Anina's words from beyond the grave clanged like a clear bell: *We must decide if creation is good or evil and act accordingly.* Hava was right. All

206

that had gone before brought us to this moment, and we must answer the call, God's own call, to hasten the coming reign of God.

And so, we came down from the mountain and slipped into Damascus in the dead of night.

I could not budge the door to Mother's home that was now bolted from the inside. I knocked, but not too loud, and soon I heard rustling within, the iron lock clanged open, and lamplight spilled through a crack in the door.

"Mother meet your daughter," I said. "Wife meet your mother."

The elder woman with streaks of gray hair was not surprised at the sun-tanned woman who basked in the yellow glow of the oil lamp, and Mother grabbed my bride and pulled her inside, kissed her forehead, then wrapped both arms around her and squeezed tight as they swayed from side to side. I removed the oil lamp from her hand before it spilled or set us afire and quietly bolted the door behind us.

The bleating of the goats and the aroma of Mother's loaves browning on the hearth gently roused me from my dreams. I tugged at the wool blanket to cover my sleeping wife's nakedness, and then I poured water into a basin and splashed my face awake before joining my mother outside. She sat on a squat stool and tugged at the teats of a she-goat, and I stood quietly behind her and listened to the rhythmic squish, squish of goat's milk squirting into a bowl. When I leaned over and kissed the top of her head, she reached her hand back and stroked my cheek. She handed me a piece of hot flat bread with honey that dribbled into my beard, which she wiped away with a corner of her apron.

"I am so happy," she said, and the smile in her eyes said the same. "And such a beautiful wife!"

"And such a beautiful mother!" Hava replied from the doorway.

We all moved inside and sat around the oak table that bore the etchings from my youth. We ate our fill of fresh bread and honey washed down with warm goat's milk. I watched with great interest at the immediate affection between the two women in my life, but then a shadow settled over the table when Hava asked, "Is there any news of my parents and the young child?"

Mother pursed her lips and shook her head.

It seemed that Yosef, Hannah, Rahab, and Ahuva, the deaf-mute girl, disappeared the same day that King Agrippa stole Yosef's livestock. I hoped they heeded my warning and sought sanctuary from the reprisals that were sure to come after I had rescued Hava from the king. But where?

Later that day, Hava and I borrowed horses from Rufus and Alexander and rode out to the encampment outside the city. A few tattered and broken-down tents remained, but the place had been ransacked, and scavengers left no clue as to the fate of my in-laws. The anxiety of unknowing would be a prickly reminder that doom remained near, a threat reinforced by the overt hostility that bubbled up between the precincts and peoples of Damascus. Rather than thwarting my eagerness of purpose, the menace of lurking death and destruction, for which Jerusalem was merely a cipher, only strengthened my resolve and added urgency to my call to tell the good news.

The next morning, I announced my intention to spend the day with the holy scrolls of old at the synagogue.

"Today, you may do so," Hava replied. "But do not expect to study alone. This is something we will do together. We will be a team, melding my tradition as a Jewish follower of Yeshua in his homeland with your Iesou traditions from the Hellenist congregations." She reached and clasped Mother's hand. "But today I will spend with my mother, and she will tell me what a naughty child you were." Mother and daughter shared a conspiratorial smile.

In the snippets I collected about the man from Nazareth, two themes recurred. "Who do you say that I am?" --a question that he never answered--and his constant preaching and parables about the reign of God. It only made sense that these should be the organizing principles of my narrative. I had long believed that the messianic expectations of a warrior-king who would lead God's people to military victory offered false hope, a misunderstanding that even the Nazarene leadership shared, and my narrative must counter this confusion. What then was the nature of this son of man, son of David, son of God, the anointed one, the mashiah, the christos?

My dear wife, whose reading primer had been these same old scrolls from the library of her Pharisee grandfather, constantly referred to the prophet Esaias.

"The key is the extraordinary intimacy between Iesou and God," she would remind me. "The prophets, especially Esaias, spoke God's promise that one would come who would have an unprecedented relationship with him, who would redeem his people, and who would restore Eden and God's good creation."

But here was the paradox. The one to come would not be a holy warrior, and redemption would not come through holy war. He would be a healer and not a conqueror. Broken relationships would be restored--among individuals, between whole peoples, and with God through forgiveness rather than judgment, through love rather than strife. The way of the Lord, promised by Esaias, would be that of a suffering servant. This would be the one whose story we would tell.

Surely, he has borne our infirmities and carried our diseases; yet we accounted him stricken, struck down by God, and afflicted. But he was wounded for our transgressions, crushed for our iniquities; upon him was the punishment that made us whole, and by his bruises we are healed.

And what of death's riddle? The cross had been his end and perhaps would be ours as well. What is life's meaning in the face of death? Death had come near me often: my first wife and child, the Roman aquilifer by my own hand, Rehum's death that preserved my own life, and the most senseless of all--the rape and murder of Anina. Is life merely an illusion, and death the reality? Or, is there more? Death was a mystery that I could not solve, but was there not hope in the empty tomb? There could be no other ending for my narrative save the climactic events in Jerusalem when Iesou was arrested, tried, convicted, and executed but raised and missing from the place they had laid him; my entire storyline must presage these last days.

But where to begin? Best to get a problem out of the way right at the outset: Iesou was a disciple--an underling--to Yochanan the baptizer, and the ministry of Iesou began only after Yochanan had been imprisoned. My retelling of the baptism of Iesou in the River Jordan must be carefully crafted, to clarify the role of Yochanan as prophet, as the last and greatest, certainly the most immediate, proclaimer of God's promise to send one "in the name of the Lord." In his baptism, Iesou was claimed as God's own and called to proclaim God's reign. We would rely on traditions of the miraculous to heighten the impact of this adoption of the man from Nazareth to fulfill God's redemptive purpose.

The summer months passed too quickly, and events passed me by. I happened to be working alone at the synagogue when the news flashed through the streets and alleys of Damascus; on the ninth day of the late-summer month of Av, the Jerusalem temple had fallen, and the ruin of Jerusalem had been realized. Tens of thousands had been slaughtered. I left my pen and inks and the scribbles on my scrolls scattered on the synagogue floor and hurried home.

I flung open the door and blurted out the news, but my mother put a finger to her lips and said, "Sit and enjoy a bowl of lamb stew."

Though I was perplexed, I did as she suggested. I removed my skull cap and beat the dust from my robe as my wife entered from the back stoop. With her hands clasping my cheeks, she kissed me on the mouth. Even in the dim light of the oil lamps, her eyes sparkled, and the curled corners of her mouth hinted at a smile that teased but never quite appeared.

Mother placed a bowl of steaming lamb stew in front of me. Hava slid the plate of flat loaves to the side of the stew then poured a bowl of beer for me. They watched me tear off a hunk of bread and sop it in my stew.

"What?" I said, suddenly aware that something was amiss. "Why don't you sit? What's going on?"

Mother nodded at Hava. With tears streaming down her nut-brown cheeks, Hava's suppressed smile burst across her face.

"You're going to be a papa," she said.

Chapter Twenty-eight

A ghost appeared in Damascus and threatened my wife and unborn child and the serenity that had nestled upon our lives. Festering wounds and half-healed scars marred the gaunt apparition's face and arms. Abner, the former husband to my wife, was dead in Jerusalem, we believed, but now his specter limped out of the morning mist following autumn rains.

"Stop, scribe." The unholy voice chilled me as I ascended the steps to the synagogue. "Take me to my wife."

If I carried a sword, I might have hacked the menace that jeopardized my happy existence right then and there; since I was not armed, my impulse was to run to my love, to carry her off to our mountain hideaway, and to never speak of this encounter with the man who first claimed her heart, but I was frozen in place, and my mouth opened and shut without any sound escaping save an anguished wheeze.

"Take me to my wife," the man insisted as he grasped my arm with a bony grip.

"She is no longer your wife," I barely whispered.

"Yes, so I heard. She has taken a lowly scribe, but she is of higher station than that." He spoke of me as if I wasn't present.

I shook his hand loose from my arm as my courage swelled along with my resentment of the haughty fool who had once abandoned dear Hava to fight a hopeless cause, but I still worried about her reaction to the arrival of the husband we thought dead. Again, I considered stealing her away, or leading him in the wrong direction, but I knew she must decide, and I would trust her in that, and so, I brought him to her.

"Oh, dear Abner," she said as she filled a basin and washed the grime from his wounds and applied her healing unguent.

My own mother also fawned over my challenger. "Tell us of Jerusalem," she implored as she set a tall goblet of wine and loaves of flat bread on the table in front of him. He drank deeply and wolfed down the loaves before he spoke.

"Passover," he said as he began to relive the destruction of Jerusalem. "Our doom was decreed on Passover. Instead of sending plagues on the Romans as God had done to the Egyptians, instead of passing over as God had passed over the houses with lamb's blood on the lentil and doorposts, instead of swallowing up our enemies as God had done in the Red Sea, the Lord God Almighty stood by as the Romans encircled the city and began their assault."

Once again, he spit out the word, "Passover." The disillusioned and despairing man had lost his faith.

"First came the famine. Children with bloated bellies and vacant eyes wandered alone in the empty marketplace. Food had already been scarce, but when the Romans cut off all entry into the city, the scarcity mounted by day and so too the suspicions, resentments, and thievery among the populace. If so much as a crumb should appear, brother set upon brother. Why, there were even stories of cannibalism … too grotesque to repeat."

His voice trailed off as his face suddenly blanched, and I feared he would retch the bread he had eaten. He interrupted his tale and stepped into the fresh air of the courtyard until his color returned.

"The starving children owed their fate to the zealot rebels who intentionally burned the granaries and bins of corn that had been laid up! Can you believe it?" Abner's voice trailed off, and he paused to let his words sink in as he shook his head and made clucking sounds with his tongue.

213

"Some said it was done to force God's hand and compel divine intervention to save Jerusalem—if so, God intervened alright, but on the side of the Romans. More likely, it was jealous animosity between the zealot leaders, Eleazar ben Simon and John of Gischala."

I cringed inwardly as regret pierced my heart and spilled my shame at the hearing of the names of the tyrants who had once been my masters.

"After their collaboration succeeded in ousting, or at least neutralizing, the aristocratic faction led by Ananus ben Ananus, the zealots turned against each other; instead of preparing for the Roman onslaught, the rebel factions clashed, and they burned the stores of food to harm the other. Can you believe it?" He repeated the hanging question without expecting an answer.

I couldn't help myself; I had to ask. "What became of Eleazar?"

"Passover." Abner answered me with newfound and curious interest, as if he noticed my presence for the first time. "I told you that our end began at Passover. So, too, did Passover decree the fate of Eleazar."

The clop, clop of the stallion's hooves on the stone courtyard nearly drowned out my thoughts as I tried to listen closely to the account of Eleazar's demise.

"Eleazar and his men controlled the temple and access to temple sacrifice, but on the 14th day of the month of Nisan, Eleazar allowed entry for those who desired to offer sacrifice in remembrance of God's actions in saving his people from the Egyptians, but hundreds of John's men infiltrated the pilgrim masses with weapons concealed beneath their robes. Once inside the temple walls, they fell upon Eleazar's unsuspecting troops and killed without resistance, including many of the innocents. It is said that Eleazar himself was struck down and died when he retreated into the innermost sanctum, the Holy of Holies, and his body, without a single blemish upon it, was burned on the altar."

News of the death of the man I once followed, then feared, and then loathed was hardly surprising, and I was neither joyful nor sad. I no longer despised him for who he was, even if he was not who we hoped he would be. I suppose there was ironic justice in his death; the audacious tyrant who profaned the temple in the first place met his end by miscalculating the gall of one more conniving than he. Such are the affairs of mortal men.

Abner picked up his story. "Soon, the Roman attacks began, and John's troops awkwardly fumbled with the ballistae and catapults Eleazar had plundered at Beth Horon years earlier for they had little skill in using these massive engines of war."

He drummed his fingers against the oak table as he remembered.

"The outer wall fell, then a second wall, and the Romans butchered everyone, not merely the combatants but peaceful citizens, women and children, the aged and infirm. None were spared, and the heaps of corpses grew higher and higher; a river of blood splashed through the gutters and poured down stairways, and the bodies of those killed at the top slithered to the bottom."

My resentment toward Abner softened with a tinge of pity as he relived the nightmare that was not a dream. His breathing quickened, and his voice rose.

"All that remained was the upper city around Herod's palace, the fortress next to the temple, and the temple itself; as spring turned to summer, the Roman battering rams assaulted the temple walls with little effect, but then the adjacent fortress fell, allowing the legionnaires a platform to heave chunks of burning wood onto the temple grounds. The

215

fires of damnation spread, and flames soon licked at the doorways to the inner courts and then consumed the Holy of Holies. Plumes of black smoke billowed to the heavens."

The man broke down and sobbed, and his shoulders heaved, and he asked in a quivering voice, "Was the aroma pleasing to the Lord?"

Mother refilled Abner's goblet with wine from a vase in the corner. He drank it down quickly. After a couple of deep breaths, he was ready to continue.

"Within weeks, the final precincts around Herod's palace fell, and I fought with the last remnant until we all died with swords in our hands—at least, I thought I perished with the others. I fell under the blows that rained upon us, and then I remember nothing until hours later or days later when I awoke amongst the piles of corpses that lay where we fell. I thought myself a ghost as I walked through the smoldering ruins and heaps of rubble from the once proud temple walls, and I just kept walking. I no longer recognized the city of God, for it was no longer a city, God had departed, and I just kept walking. There were no longer gates to the city for there were no walls, and I just kept walking. There were no longer trees or shrubs on the surrounding hills—only stumps and ash--even the Mount of Olives was laid barren, and I just kept walking."

Hava swept away the long strands of hair that drooped over his face and wiped away his tears. He lifted his face to her and spoke.

"Hava, dear Hava. I have been spared to return to you."

My own heart thumped in my chest. She took his hand in hers and looked deeply into his eyes and kissed him on the forehead.

"I am more than fond of you, dear Abner, but …"

She pulled his hand to her belly.

"Do you feel the life inside? The child who stirs within belongs to Markos, who is my husband now and the man I love."

Chapter Twenty-nine

As usual, my cooing daughter awakened me as she nuzzled her mother's breast. I changed the babe's soiled clothing and rocked her in my arms before passing her back to her mother.

After eating my own breakfast, I kissed my wife on the lips and my daughter on her thick-matted, black-haired head. She briefly released her mother's breast and whimpered before latching on again, and then I hustled off to the synagogue to prepare for the gathering of the congregation later.

It was the first day of the week and the culmination of the high Hebrew holy days known as Passover that remembered the rescue of God's people from Egypt, but our synagogue would focus upon those fateful days when Iesou was arrested and crucified four decades earlier. Today would mark the first time that our congregation would celebrate with a new narrative--scribed by my own hand--centered not on the passover and the exodus, but on the life and passion of Iesou. Then, to complete this splendid day, our daughter would be welcomed into the community through the rite of baptism.

Although the morning sun illuminated the expansive room quite well, I lit clay lamps filled with olive oil and set them atop tables and on wall extrusions built for that purpose. I nervously glanced over my scroll and placed it on the Torah shrine in the middle of the floor, ready for its first public reading. Alexander dropped by and mysteriously suggested he would be late for the service, but in my busyness, I didn't really pay attention.

By midday, the first congregants began to arrive. I recognized many old faces who remembered me as a youngster underfoot, but there were many newcomers as well. Rufus, his wife, and two children arrived early and claimed seats in the first row of the stone benches, right in front of the Torah shrine. Hava and my mother and daughter soon joined them, and they saved a seat for me, while I wandered about the room, greeting the arrivals. We held a place for Alexander and his family, but their seats remained empty as the synagogue hall filled. Finally, his wife and three children appeared but still no Alexander, and his wife wouldn't make eye contact with me. Three rows of stone seats lined each side of the hall and a balcony with a standing area encircled the entire room. I had never seen the old hall so full; word had spread that we would unveil new readings of our own and not lessons borrowed from our Hebrew past. By the appointed time, the congregants had spilled to the floor because all the seats were full.

Abner was one of these, standing near the door. I knew that he attended out of curiosity more than belief, but as his physical and emotional wounds healed, he became inquisitive; on his best days, he dared to hope.

The world had turned. Only a single wall remained of the once glorious temple in Jerusalem, and the shining city on a hill had been reduced to rubble coated with soot and ash. There wasn't a Jew among us who hadn't lost a cousin, or an uncle, or a brother, or their whole family in the Roman onslaught. Vespasian now sat on the emperor's throne in Rome, and his son, General Titus, was mopping up against the few remaining zealots who had taken refuge in the desert far to the south of Jerusalem in the cliffs of Masada. The old had fallen away, but the new had not yet arrived, and we were an anxious lot; I was about to speak to that anxiety, but first I needed to calm my own nerves, and I gulped down a cup of water.

219

As I rose to my feet to take my place at the Torah shrine, Alexander's empty seat in front of me momentarily jarred me, but I cleared my throat and instinctively reached for my reed pen behind my ear. The familiar touch was reassuring.

Toward the end of the narrative, we had planned an interlude for the breaking of the bread and the drinking of the wine, a ritual that had long been the centerpiece of our communal gatherings. From my scroll, I read these words:

"He took a loaf of bread, and after blessing it he broke it, gave it to them, and said, "Take; this is my body." Then he took a cup, and after giving thanks he gave it to them, and all of them drank from it."

At that point, appointed helpers began to distribute bread and wine from the table that held the vases and loaves. They had nearly finished when Alexander finally entered from the back door, but he was not alone; a Roman soldier accompanied him. The room hushed, and the crowd parted to allow them to proceed toward me, and I remembered the words of the old follower of Yochanan the baptizer during our caravan journey: "Speak the truth, whatever the cost," and I thought of the broken body of Anina and of Iesou hanging on the cross. Abner unsheathed a sword and took a couple of steps forward, ready to continue his war against the Romans, if necessary.

The soldier was tall and muscled. His *gladius* and his *pugio* remained sheathed. When he reached me, he extended both hands and cupped them. His blue eyes were moist, and his bare blond head bowed slightly.

"Please, may I eat of the bread?"

After all had eaten, the congregation sang a hymn, and Hava joined me in the center of the hall for the baptism. I held our child in my arms as Hava splashed water over the babe's head.

Just then, the double doors burst open, and the late afternoon sun flooded the entrance with light. All eyes turned to the doorway that opened toward the ruins of Jerusalem. Out of the brightness came a blurred figure, a child running toward us with arms wide. Hava gasped as Ahuva leaped into her arms. Others came forward: Rahab, the child's adoptive mother, Yosef, with the broadest grin ever, and Hannah, my mother-in-law, who immediately took her granddaughter from my arms and planted a wet kiss on the child's forehead. Two figures remained standing near the doors, and I squinted in the sunlight to make out Mishael and young Mattithyahu, the surviving family of Iesou, who delivered my kin from their safe sanctuary in Antioch.

****

Cold stone walls of a bone box pressed in upon a jumble of thigh bones, ribs, skulls, and tiny ivory bits from fingers and toes. Some were cracked, broken, or chipped--others worn smooth where joints had rubbed together. Here were bones of martyrs: warriors, yes, but also murdered mothers and grandmothers, slaughtered children and grandchildren. Worms had slowly devoured their decaying flesh before these remains had been packed into this bone box, their immediate resting place on the road to eternity. Dozens of the dead, perhaps more, had been squeezed into this one ossuary, and hollow eye sockets of countless skulls stared blankly into nothingness.

221

Why am I here with them? Am I not flesh and blood? Is death's rot oozing over my own skin? How long before my own bones turn brittle and then into tiny specks of dust? And what would come after that?

A mortal, born of woman, few of days and full of trouble, comes up like a flower and withers, flees like a shadow and does not last.

And what of the blood moon that pours out upon Jerusalem through the night and the smoke that blackens the sun by day? Dust and ash and suffocating fear choke the stale air inside death's chamber, and I labor to breathe. I lick my chalky lips with a thick tongue. Are these the end of days?

I hear a rattle of bone against bone. Do the bones shift? Do restless spirits stir within?

I want to cry out with them, for them ... and, for myself. "No, this cannot be! This must not be!" Certainly, our maker intended more than misery, more than injustice, indeed ... more than death.

Against all reason, I dare to hope, and that is why I have been sent here: to bolster the courage of these forlorn souls, to uplift and inspire, to instill trust and restore meaning even amid death and dying.

I unroll a papyrus scroll of my own making with ink strokes still damp, and I begin to read aloud the words I had writ for this very moment:

The beginning of the good news of Iesou Christos ...

Beams of light filtered through the dust that hung in the stale air. The bones in the stone ossuary fused together. Skulls rested atop vertebrae, and the tiny ebony bits became fingers and toes. Full skeletons appeared before me now, and hair sprouted from the crowns of many skulls. I unfurled more and more of my scroll, and I continued to read aloud.

Mottled flesh appeared as faces, muscles and sinews formed arms and legs, and eye sockets were filled with rheumy white eyes. Young men and old, heavy-set women and thin, all leaned in with pricked ears and listened. I see trouble on their faces. Furrowed brows. Tears dripping down cheeks. Downturned lips. Why must we suffer? Why must we die? Meaning is elusive, I know, and yet I must attempt an answer.

Bright light and fresh air filled the hall as sunbeams slanted through open windows, and the breeze bore the scent of spring flowers. The congregation in front of me milled about, anxious yet hopeful. I have come down the mountain to share the good news with them that God meets us in our flesh through Iesou our brother. If Iesou is beloved, so too are you and me!

I know these faces! There is Simon, the long-dead father of Rufus and Alexander standing next to my own departed father. And my dead wife cuddling our child. And the aquilifer that I killed, clutching the golden eagle close. Rehum listens with a gruff face but a sparkle in his eye. Happy tears dribble down the smiling face of Anina. And so many more; the walls of the room are gone, and hundreds, thousands, tens of thousands of souls are in the congregation that hears these words.

"As they entered the tomb, they saw a young man, dressed in a white robe, sitting on the right side; and they were alarmed. But he said to them, 'Do not be alarmed; you are looking for Jesus of Nazareth, who was crucified. He has been raised; he is not here.'"

223

From the Author

Thank you for reading my book. If you enjoyed it, won't you please take a moment to leave a review at your favorite retailer?

You can also leave a comment on my personal website. www.rwholmen.com.

I'm a descendant of Scandinavian immigrants who eventually found their way to a farming community in Central Minnesota near the end of the 19th century. My paternal great-grandparents settled a few miles north of the town of Upsala, and my maternal great-grandparents settled a few miles south of town. Members of both families remained until my parents married and moved off the farm and into town where Dad became a successful small-town businessman. I was baptized and confirmed in the same Swedish-Lutheran church that nurtured my grandmother and mother.

I experienced a glorious childhood in Upsala in the '50s and '60s. Bike riding, ball playing, pony riding, and especially fishing and water-skiing on nearby Cedar Lake where G-pa and G-ma Holmen lived in the lakeside retirement home they built. When high school rolled around, I was active in sports, and when I was honored as valedictorian of my forty-two-person graduating class, I was merely following family tradition after three of Dad's sisters, Mom's sister, and Mom herself had been valedictorians before me.

In the fall of '66, I was off to Dartmouth, but within two years, I arrived in Vietnam as Neil Armstrong walked on the moon. On Christmas eve 1970, I was discharged in time to return to Dartmouth for the start of winter term. Following Dartmouth, I endured the paper chase of law school at the University of Minnesota before becoming a trial attorney in St. Cloud, Minnesota.

In the early '90s while continuing my law practice, I studied with the Benedictine monks at the nearby St. John's School of Theology where I discovered a keen interest in the history behind the formation of the Biblical canon. Who were the authors? What were the circumstances that influenced them? For whom were their writings intended?

Years later, my interest in Paul, the principal author of the Christian New Testament, resulted in publication of *A Wretched Man, a novel of Paul the Apostle*. Readers sang the novel's praises. "Regardless of your personal religious background, this book is absolutely breathtaking." "The novel was difficult to put down and brought to life a distant time and place with such humanity and liveliness." Academic reviewers praised the historical authenticity of the novel's treatment of the lives and times of the first generation of the Christian church.

My experiences as an army Ranger scouting the jungles of the Central Highlands of Vietnam serve as inspiration for my bold, dark, and intense novella entitled *Gonna Stick My Sword in the Golden Sand*. One reviewer suggested the book was "not merely a war story but a story of life and choices."

For years, I followed the struggle of LGBTQ Christians to be fully accepted by their churches, and when my own Lutheran denomination changed their policies during their national convention in Minneapolis in 2009, I was there as a "graceful engagement" volunteer. *Queer Clergy, A History of Gay and Lesbian Ministry in American Protestantism*, remembers the queer prophets and celebrates the journey toward full

225

inclusion. This non-fiction book was a finalist for a Minnesota Book Award.

More recently, I have returned to early church history and the tumultuous 1st century that saw a Jewish revolt against Roman imperialism. *Wormwood and Gall: The Destruction of Jerusalem and the First Gospel* remembers the context but fictionalizes the characters behind the "Gospel According to Mark."

I have been married to Lynn for over forty years, and we have three adult children and two granddaughters.

Friend me on Facebook: https://www.facebook.com/ObiesBookBlog/

43224310R10137

Made in the USA
Middletown, DE
23 April 2019